# January Through December

## Twelve Short Stories - One Coffee Shop

### By Audrey L. Elder

**January Through December:**
**Twelve Short Stories - One Coffee Shop**

ISBN 978-1-7378922-1-2

Illustrations:
January, June, July-- Ella Youmans

February – Anita Sisk

March, April, September, October, November, December-
Dan Hadley

May- James Elder

August- Daniel Curtis

Published by HearthMasters Publishing
PO Box 1166
Independence, MO 64050
www.hearthmasters.net

# Dedication

For Uncle Bernard. Yes, I'm still watching the bee.

# Acknowledgements

Dan, James, Melissa, Becca, Sandy, and Marge-
Your encouragement, your belief in me and your
straightforward feedback gave me the strength to
make this happen.

Amanda- Without your expertise, *January*
couldn't have sung out its story.

Liana, David, Sam, and Becca- Eight eyes and
four brilliant minds. THANK YOU for the edits
and suggestions and THANK YOU for
continuing to respond to my emails that often
have only one word in the subject line- HELP.

# Contents

# Introduction

A coffee shop is the living room of a community.

It is far from just a place to get a caffeinated drink.

It is far from inanimate.

It is alive and carries the energy of every soul that has come through its doors.

And yet, every single person becomes part of the scenery blending in with the tables and chairs, wall art and the dulled sound of white noise.

And yet, every single person is one thread of the fabric of that community. It doesn't matter if they are a lifelong resident or a transient visitor, their presence becomes a part of what is and what will be.

I met *my coffee shop* in 2009. Over the years it has become a home away from home and the source of countless friendships that will last a lifetime. As I got to know many of the people who frequent *my* java joint, I grew a better understanding of my own community. I also soon realized that only a few degrees separated each of us from each other, even without the coffee shop as a common point of geography.

I'll never forget the odd moment I shared something with a small group of friends about the day my grandfather passed away. I can't even remember what brought the story up. My grandparents had only lived in the area for ten years before he passed in 2006. One of my friends asked me what his name was. Turns out he was there in the hospital that day as a chaplain to my grandpa. He was there at the funeral. He knew my family, and to think he had become like family to me before I knew any of this. This moment created the thought, or I should say, the question that became this book. *What are the stories of the people we see every day and just how much more connected to them are we than we realize?*

Wherever I go, I find a coffee shop. I might bring in a notebook, or my computer or my most recent bound obsession. In the tiny narrow coffee shop filled with poetry books in Boulder, CO, the packed brick colonial coffee shop just blocks from Emerson, Thoreau, Alcott & Hawthorne's graves in Concord, MA, the Greek cuisine / fill your own cup shop a stones-throw from the Missouri Capitol in Jefferson City.... I read, write, sip and wonder...*what are the stories?*

An old downtown, designated as historic or not, is an ecosystem filled with buildings, streets, trees, birds, businesses, and people. When it is healthy, we refer to it as "a community." When it is decline, we say, "It has potential." The mid-century era concept that old is bad; new and modern is good still creeps into long term planning. Meanwhile, our downtowns have been left barren and often desolate like a clear-cut forest. Nearly a hundred years of suburban living and chain store shopping has created disconnected communities and fragmented economies.

I shouldn't have been surprised that I had found a personal connection with a coffee shop friend via my grandfather. I shouldn't have been surprised by any one of the connections I found with every

single person I have met while drinking coffee. I should have expected it.

I began writing this book in 2013. I finished it seven years later from the front porch of my home during the COVID-19 pandemic in the summer of 2020. The planet seemed to become quiet while we all experienced an eerie daily sense of surrealism and our favorite places closed. While *life* was on pause, I imagined myself back at the place I realized I missed the most, *my* coffee shop. I imagined that we would all get through the future page of the history books titled "2020" and emerge at least in some sense....better.

These stories, situations, and the characters therein are purely fictional outside of a few personality traits borrowed from my husband, daughter, son, and daughter-in-law. They are, however, stories you can find in any town or community in the United States...maybe beyond. Each chapter is a solitary short story of its own while interwoven in tiny threads with other chapters as the book continues.

The illustrations are from various Missouri artists. Artists of all kinds, those who draw, sing, dance, act, and even those who write all experienced disproportionate financial hardship during the pandemic. Please support your local artist with admiration and your wallet!

I hope you enjoy the book, try to support your locally owned businesses and most of all....tip your barista!!

Audrey L Elder

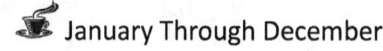 January Through December

# 1

# January

Michael whispered as his hand clutched her jacket sleeve, "Cass, watch your step, glass."

"Babe, I can't see anything."

"Get on my back."

Glass crunched softly under Michael's hiking boots. They moved upwards then around two corners until he let her down at a step of stairs. "Can you hold me? Can you feel the steps?"

"Yeah, I think so. Let's go."

The sun was just beginning to think about arriving. This was the shot he was after. The full moon and the rising sun, all at once. A sort of Ansel Adams tribute, except the scene wasn't nature's best, it was humanity's worst. And yet, to Michael, every abandoned building held a story. A story of a dream gone wrong or forgotten. The idea of getting the perfect shot of the sun rising as the moon still hung bright in the sky was a way of reminding us that despite our decisions, right or wrong, the world kept turning.

They reached the top of the stairs just in time. Michael whipped the tripod and both cameras out of his backpack. He really was an Adams fan. Cass breathed in deeply as the clicks of dueling shutters began to capture the moment. She carefully sipped the coffee from the mug she had filled just half an hour before. By the time she had pulled her notebook and pen from her own backpack, the sun, that infamous sun had begun to seep its beautiful light near enough that she could seize the moment in her own way as he did his.

*He captured the sun and the moon which both rose above this place that once sent men home so dirty the detergent wars were born. Yet so dirty, mortgages were paid, savings accounts were created, and retirements were confirmed.*

A simple kiss and the two were off to take in as much of the insides of the forgone factory as could be found. Michael shot as he walked. Sharp grey edges of fallen frame, the shape of the bottom of a coffee cup etched into an old bent and faded green metal desk, half opened lockers that swayed slightly with each gust of wind that poured through the old break room.

"How much time do I have?" he asked Cass as he set his tripod in front of a giant rusted machine.

"It's 6:30, we should leave by 7:00."

"Perfect, just two more rooms. I'll be done in twenty."

3

The coffee shop was warm, dark, and silent. Cass took her usual seat in the back corner where she could work on her computer and see everyone arrive. Michael began to bring the shop to life.

With only enough light to illuminate the back of the bar, he methodically began measuring the current menu blends; a signature dark roast, a seasonal Chocolate Spice, and a reduced-acid decaf. He carefully filled the filters in the large stainless-steel pots with the fresh aromatic grounds. The routine was invariable, turn the lights on the cooler below the outside of the bar. Fill it with flavored waters, sandwiches, fruit cups and hummus snack packs. Put out cream, sugars, honey, and cinnamon. Check napkin dispensers. Count the register, fill the sanitizer, and soap sinks, turn on the television and music and finally.... flip the open sign.

Michael grabbed two large coffee cups from the counter and filled them both with Chocolate Spice. He leaned back into the chair next to Cass breathing in the steaming scent of nutmeg, "ready for another day."

The television caught Cass's eye. Silently it poured the words of the news networks continuous "BREAKING NEWS" in broken white letters amid a black box that hung over the top of the screen. *Look, he inherited this situation. He's got two years to pass legislation that can create some resemblance of a fix and at the same time keep the party happy.*

*Is it actually possible to pull that off in two years?*

*A Band-Aid, maybe. He'll have strong opposition in the House and being the opposing majority, he's going to have to compromise. I guarantee they're already planning the attack ads.*

The faint charming ding of the entrance doorbell rang right on time, 7:06 am.

"Hi Lewis!" Michael called out to the umbrella shaking man in the plain gray suit.

"Good morning, Michael, that rain came out of nowhere."

"Yeah, Cass and I had clear skies for this morning's outing, I had no idea it was going to rain."

Lewis waved his hand to Cass, "Morning Lewis" she called from the back corner.

"The usual?"

"Yep, and as usual, to go. Another fun windowless day in the cubie." He laughed, but he meant

5

it. He hated it and at the same time convinced himself daily that he was the luckiest man on earth. The benefits though, a two-year contract, and just a few years to retirement to go do whatever it was he always dreamed of, although when asked he seemed to have forgotten what that dream was. "Got big weekend plans?"

Michael put the final touches on the vanilla cappuccino, "Cass is still working on Saturdays. He whispered, "I'm going to surprise her and bring lunch though on her late break."

Lewis looked sad, but he had dedicated to *sacrifice* himself in life. "That my friend is why she loves you." Lewis tossed a five-dollar bill on the counter, took his cappuccino, and left.

Just like clockwork, by 8:15 Michael's manager Elena came through the back door with the day's fresh pastries. By 8:20, Olivia was behind the counter just as a line began to form. Cass loved mornings at the coffee shop. The variety of people who came through the front door intrigued her. She imagined what their lives were like, what was on their minds, where they went once a cup with a cardboard ring and a plastic lid entered their hands. There were middle aged men in suits, moms in yoga pants and winter hoodies that pushed a stroller meant to double as a treadmill. Young hipsters with Zen

tattoos, big colorful bags, and intellectual beards. The office-less self-employed with a laptop backpack and a constant check of the clock for a meeting that would hopefully end with a contract. The khaki pants badge wearers who she was sure, at least for the most part, picked a career that would provide a sense of purpose. The politicians that became regulars about a month before the primaries then seemed to disappear for the next couple years. The group of retired women who took the big round center table to share pictures of their grandkids and European vacations. The group of new moms who met in the delivery wing of the hospital and decided to keep in touch forever. The visitors, the tourists, the conference attendees- always in awe of each moment. The homeless who were cold and hungry. The lost who were simply lonely.

Often people knew each other, visiting in the line or stopping by a table to say hello. Most though, seemed to be in a world of their own immersed in their laptops, conversations, or a constant scrolling of a smart phone. Cass knew some of their stories. Michael knew many more. Though the atmosphere was always in a state of evolution, to Cass it felt like the one place that *community* was exemplified, or at least held the potential to be so.

9:30 a.m., her phone sang a gentle sound akin to a bamboo wind chime. She packed up her computer and notebook, drank the last sip of coffee from her cup and made her way to the end of the counter. "Off to work babe" she called just loud enough for Michael to hear her, "I'll be back by 4:30."

Michael flipped the steam wand of the espresso machine into a tiny pitcher of water and made a quick dash to kiss her goodbye.

Elena handed him a slip of paper the second he returned with the next order to fill, "Your car is still broke, huh?"

"It's the transmission. We're going to my parents' tonight to borrow the family beater until we can save up enough to fix it."

"At least you have that option."

"Yeah, totally. I'm grateful, I'm just not entirely looking forward to the dinner that will inevitably be followed by a lecture before I get to borrow the car."

"Just how parents show their love sometimes."

Michael laughed as he reached into the mini fridge for the soy milk. "That's fair."

The rain had turned to sleet before turning to snow. Tiny white frozen beads falling straight out of the sky as having been poured from a saltshaker. The car was still warm from Cass driving in. Michael grabbed the handle of the passenger door expecting it to be locked. He gently tapped on the window which startled Cass causing her to slam the book in her hands shut and dive across the console to unlock the door. "You ready?" She asked with slight sarcasm.

"Yep. You?"

"Heck yeah! It's spaghetti night! Scenic route?"

"Please."

The drive to Michael's parents was less than half an hour via the main highway, but the backroads held the sights of rolling hills covered in stubbles of corn stalks and groves of woods that promised the possibility of seeing a deer or a turkey.

Michael leaned closer to the windshield, "Take a left up here, right before the grade school."

Cass flipped the blinker. It ticked loudly as if to announce something more important than a left turn. She stopped the car at the sign, waited her turn and slowly, not knowing why, turned onto a little winding road. Michael kept glued to the windshield as the mid-century blocky brick of the grade school faded into a neighborhood of little split levels and tiny ranch homes set just far enough apart from each other to create a sense of personal space for their residents.

"Follow the curve. Don't go straight." He continued to narrate his secretive navigation.

Past the curve the lots became bigger. The houses became bigger and set further and further back from the road. The bigger the lot, the larger the outbuildings. The largest proudly displayed long rows of solar panels and all had a faded or algae covered propane tank near the house. After a solid mile Cass stopped at a stop sign. Michael sat back.

"Here. Look." He pointed out her side window. "I've always loved this house."

Cass checked her rearview mirror. No one was behind her, so she stared. A little red brick bungalow with an inviting covered porch was Michael's entire reason for the off-highway route. Despite the cold air he rolled his window down to get a better view, "Cass, if you could live anywhere, would you want to stay living in town or live somewhere like this?"

A large truck was quickly making its way toward them. "I have to go, the truck."

Michael pointed to the right, "This will get us back to the highway."

The demanding blinker returned just long enough for Cass to turn onto the kind of road that at any amount of speed could double as a roller coaster ride. "You know, it's tempting Michael. I mean the idea of having a big clump of dirt. Space to grow a giant garden, have chickens, a few fruit trees. But on the same hand I love that we can walk or bike to go wherever we want from our apartment. We know everyone. Yeah, that's a tough one."

"I pretty much feel the same way. I struggle with that."

"Until we're done with school and get better jobs and get...married, we can put this in the maybe box!"

"Good point. Hey, speaking of which, how was work today? I meant to ask earlier. Guess I got caught up in the drive."

Cass laughed, "It was fine. You know I can't talk about it."

"Babe, it's me. Who am I gonna tell?"

11

"Okay, no names though."

"Deal."

"I worked with a couch hopper today. It was actually really awful. I mean this kid is so driven, he wants to go to college so bad. He's one of the top players on his basketball team and sometimes he ends up having to walk three miles in the dark after school to the house he's staying at after practice. They've given him two weeks to find another place to stay. It's so frustrating because he isn't technically homeless. You know, as in he doesn't live on the streets so there isn't much I can do for him. It doesn't make any fricking sense."

"Does he have family?"

"His dad is in prison on a drug possession charge, his mom took his two younger siblings with her to Texas. She has a sister there that put them up. He's a senior, so this is it for him."

"At least he found you."

"And I can't do anything. I'm an intern without a voice."

"That'll change. Your voice is going to change people's lives."

"It's spaghetti time."

Cass found a spot to park as close to the house as possible somewhat in line with Michael's dad's truck, his mom's minivan, the old farm truck, the tractor and the maroon 1996 four door Chevy Impala they would take home with them at the end of the evening. Before they could open the car doors they were greeted by a howling, barking four-year-old beagle named Sadie. Michael had picked her out himself his first summer home from college. He slowly opened his door, "Hey Sadie girl! How's my girl? How's my pretty puppy?"

A voice rang out from the barn adjacent to the house and lightly graveled parking area, "That's no puppy Michael!" Mr. Albright stepped just a few feet outside the barn doors, "Good thing you're here, I need some help in here."

He turned to Cass in resignation, "You go on inside, who knows what he's up to."

Cass laughed as she reached into the back seat to grab a small paper bag. "I'll help your mom in the kitchen, like I always do. Maybe I'll learn something...not!"

Michael opened the door enough for Sadie to reach half her shaking body into the car, "wait, what's in the bag?"

"*The Giver*, you know the movie. Kayla already read the first two of the series I got her for Christmas. I promised I would buy her the movie after she read the book."

"Oh Cass, mom and dad are still recovering from you buying her those in the first place."

"She's thirteen years old. I'm building up awesome future sister-in-law points here. I'll be all incognito about it okay?"


Mr. Albright yelled once again as he retreated back into the barn, "You gonna help me or sit in that car all night?"

"On my way dad."

Michael and Sadie strolled off to the barn while Cass and her controversial gift made their way to the small porch covered in unlit Christmas lights stapled along the railing and over the door. She knocked once then slowly cracked the door open, "Hello!!"

Mrs. Albright beckoned her in from the kitchen. "Come on in!"

The house smelled like cedar and fresh bread. Kayla sprung from the living room couch dropping an Eighth Grade Earth Science book from her lap to greet Cass with a giant hug. Cass slyly slipped the bag to Kayla's hands whispering, "No need to announce this, but I promised."

"Thank you!" She smiled with her eyes squinted and whispered, "Off to my room it goes."

Mrs. Albright stood over a stock pot of boiling water with a handful of thin spaghetti noodles breaking them in half and dropping them into the pot. "And how are you dear?" She asked nearly violently stirring the little sticks of pasta as they melted into the heat.

"I'm great. Long day, but isn't every day?"

"Oh, usually. Laid off right now. Did Michael tell you?"

Cass took a seat at the kitchen table with its red apple patterned vinyl tablecloth, teacup plate of a half stick of butter and a Mr. and Mrs. Goose salt and pepper set. "He did, I just didn't realize it had started already." Cass was good at recovering in such situations.

"Started yesterday. But so far it looks like it'll only last two/three weeks, so half pay and a little time off, maybe I'll finally get the basement organized."

"Then it'll be back to work with mandatory overtime huh?"

Mrs. Albright laughed, "I sure hope so! Hey, can you put the parmesan and the salad dressings on the table?"

"I'm on it."

That's how it always went when they visited the Albrights. Michael ended up in the barn helping his dad with the latest *project*, while Cass fulfilled meaningless tasks in the kitchen with his mom. Neither minded, for all four it was how they connected and bonded.


The microwave beeped. Mrs. Albright opened the oven, pulled the loaf of garlic and butter-soaked Italian bread out and carefully set it on a giant wooden cutting board on the counter. "Kayla!!!!"

"What????"

"Go tell Nathan to bring your dad and Michael in for dinner."

"Okay."

No one walked into another room to communicate at the Albright home. They just used their loudest outside voice. Cass joked that Michael should join the theater; he had a lifetime of experience in how to project.

Michael's seventeen-year-old brother Nathan tromped from his room through the kitchen, shoulders down, eyes rolled, straight to the camo rubber boots next to the wood stove, one pant leg in, one scrunched near the top. He said nothing as he slipped on a dark green Carhart coat and headed out the door without touching the zipper.

Michael and Mr. Albright busted through the front door carrying on about the cost of replacing a motor versus the time and cost of rebuilding one. Nathan trailed in behind with an armload of firewood dropping it haphazardly on the hardwood floor next to the woodstove. "Chores done" he yelled as he kicked the boots off to nearly the same spot he had put them on.

The motor conversation continued through the living room into the kitchen. Mrs. Albright pointed her finger at them with a pre-dinner demand "wash those hands!" Words like *rotor, brushes,* and *terminals* didn't skip a beat as Michael turned the water on the kitchen sink and poured dish soap into his cupped hands. Silence ensued upon everyone taking their seat at the table, each staring at their own empty gold butterfly edged Corelle plate. Mr. Albright removed the Bass Pro cap from his head and hung it on the back of his chair. "Lord, bless this food, the beautiful hands that made it and the gift of having Cass and Michael with us tonight." A mumbled chorus of *Amens* followed before the passing of pasta, sauce, salad, and bread.

"You know Michael, you got some talent fixing things son. You could make a good living at that. I ran into a buddy of mine at the gas station today and he said the caves are hiring a couple small engine repairman."

"Thanks dad, seriously. But I got it all figured out. I'll have my master's next year, and Cass will have hers in four. One of the guys that graduated last May is already making $40,000 a year."

"And how much does he have in student debt? $40,000 a year doesn't leave much to live on if you owe $100,000 in loans. Your father and I have done just fine without pieces of paper."

"Mom, this is what I want to do. What we want to do. According to my math we should both be able to be debt free in 5-7 years as long as we also keep working and live the simple life."

Nathan couldn't help himself, "I honestly don't care about your plans or your simple life. I'd rather you got into debt and bought a car that works. Do you have any idea how embarrassing it is to ride the bus to school when you're a senior?" Mrs. Albright smacked her middle child in the arm, "watch it."

Michael quickly replied, "Dude, I'm sorry. And yeah, I do. If you remember it took me six months to get ye' olde' jalopy to run and I had to ride the bus until the end of my senior year."

Cass changed the subject. "Great dinner Donna. I still need you to teach me how to make this sauce."

"It's venison. That's what it's all about, great hamburger meals come from deer burger."

"You kids make sure you take a few bags home with you tonight. We got plenty."

"Thanks dad."

Cass smiled at Mr. Albright as she mentally conjured up the cost of what two pounds of hamburger would cost at the grocery store, "Thank you Troy, we really appreciate that."

19

Cass managed to turn the conversation to Donna's layoff, Kayla's reading club at school, Nathan's weekend job at the MFA and Troy's new distribution route. It ended with the subject of exactly when crappie season might start.

Mrs. Albright and the girls got the leftovers put away, the dishes in the dishwasher and the pots and pans washed. It was dark. The countryside had gone to sleep. The tv was turned on. It was time for Cass and Michael to go home.

---

Cass loved the view of the apartment after dark. Nothing but the glow of ten feet of LED dragonfly lights hanging over the kitchen bay window. Michael silently put the cottage cheese containers filled with spaghetti leftovers in the fridge then stepped into the bedroom to put on sweatpants and grab his laptop. Cass popped the cork of a bottle of Pinot Grigio her sister got her for Christmas. She carried the two mismatched thrift store wine glasses, each half filled into the living room. "Babe, nothing good comes from thoughts of scarcity."

"I know Cass, I know." He pushed the top of the laptop down, "Everything comes from gratitude. Please, my capacity for gratitude is a little challenged right now."

Cass pulled a soft grey fleece blanket off the back of their pink and yellow rose covered 1980's couch. "Two and a half years from today and we'll be walking down the aisle. Then, Scotland! India and Tibet!

"Then a mini-Cass and a mini-Michael. A three bedroom, two and a half bath house in a cookie cutter suburb, an SUV, a job I hate, followed by karate practice and gymnastics. You can join the PTA and I'll start golfing on the weekends." He took a sip of wine and pulled her close. His eyes glistened as the tears leaked down his cheek.

"Our mini-Cass and Michael will live exactly where we always planned on them living. In a little house surrounded by apple trees, a vegetable garden and a giant pond filled with fish."

"It's hard to see that right now. The fact that you refuse to let it go is why I love you."

---

Cass hated split shifts but that was the world of retail. Open at seven, work until eleven, find something to do until two p.m. and work again until five. Tuesdays and Fridays were her only days not working the internship job, so they were filled with split shifts at the store. Saturdays and Sundays were a straight seven to three. She made 50 cents an hour over minimum wage, but it was better than the temp agency stint. She had tried three temp jobs only to learn they don't care about a college schedule, will send you home for weeks at a time, don't offer benefits or unemployment, don't care if you come in contact with toxic chemicals, and worse of all they make several dollars an hour off your work that you never see. Retail didn't have much more to offer except it at least was somewhat flexible with a second job and she never worried about being sent home for days on end. She was one of the lucky ones though. Years back her store was fully staffed by bored housewives who wanted nothing more than a chance to get out of the house and get a discount on *stuff* to take home to redecorate. Now, there were single moms, retirees, and high school students that staffed the store while almost none of them could buy anything in it, even with the discounts.

Cass hated that Jane, who at 32 took every shift she could get, often paying for daycare for the hours she had to sit in her car or the storage room during the off time of split shifts. She truly had no other choice. The world of living wages demanded more than a high school diploma. For Cass, the world of living wages required experience to go with a bachelor's degree. Working two days a week for the social service non-profit was her only way to a real job that would even remotely pay enough to pay off her student loans if and when she got accepted to grad school. It was into this cold January morning that she stepped from the once magnificent Craftsman home now split into four apartments with her mug of coffee in one hand, bag of lunch in the other, while her phone dinged that *pay attention to me* ding. It would be one of the only attention worthy emails she had received in at least a year.

---

Lewis arrived promptly at 7:06 a.m. The usual. "Michael, you still doing photography?"

"Yeah, uh Cass and I actually got a shoot in yesterday."

Lewis pulled a folded two-sided cardstock flyer from his pocket, "Here, tourism was passing these out yesterday."

Michael scanned for the gist of the flyer, art district contest- oil, pencil, photography, and sculpture. "Thanks Lewis! I really appreciate you thinking of me. I'll see what I've got."

A line formed. Rushes happen sporadically. The known and the unknown filter out to couches, small tables, high tops, and the edge of the pick-up counter. Their emotions; rushed, relaxed, anxious, excited, sad, impassioned. Soon the air was filled with a blend of all the above. Michael acted as the oboe tuning the orchestra. Despite the absence of a baton, a modern concerto of sounds, thoughts and feelings had created that *atmosphere* that drew them all to that place. In that moment he forgot about getting the car fixed and his class at three. In that moment he wasn't thinking about the past or the future. He caught a glimpse of this rare sense of feeling fully present. Fully immersed in life unfolding around him as a drop of water joins the rain, soon becoming a river.

Like a well-oiled machine Michael, Elena and Olivia filled the orders assembly line style calling them out for pickup in circular motion. As the last cup was filled and the final plate removed from the toaster oven, sounds once again became words, and laughter and chairs audibly scooted across the plank wood floor. Intermission.

Cass pushed the cart up and down every aisle of the grocery store. She had a list. It was a splurge and not the best time for it, however a really special meal was her go-to for bomb dropping. It was all about presentation. Not so much the food, the bomb part. So, she continued to wind along the isles. Rehearsing her thoughts followed by reminding herself that nothing should be rehearsed. Everything should simply flow. Dinner should be made with focus and concentration. Love should be the only thought on her mind. The bomb, not a bomb, the news, should be delivered with as much thoughtfulness as the meal itself.

*Everything happens for a reason.............*

*Everything happens for a reason..............*

A six pack of KC Bier Dunkel and she was off to the checkout counter. She was given a gift somewhere, somehow. Maybe it was genetic, maybe some environmental influence. Either way, her ability to accept what was, move forward and laugh at least a little never, ever failed her. She sang all the way to the car and all the way home, "Whatever will be will be, the future's not ours to see, que sera, sera."

Michael entered the living room stomping his snow-covered shoes on the estate sale braided rug that he bought just because it reminded him of his grandmother's kitchen. He carefully dropped his backpack and coat on the living room chair.

"Is it snowing?" Cass called from the kitchen.

"Just like you wished it would have for Christmas. We can do a dollar store re-do if you want."

Cass laughed, "That might actually be fun. Get in here! I made Swiss steak! Michael slowly peaked around the corner of the thick white 1920's trim that divided the living room from the kitchen. "Dammit Cass. You're an open book baby. What happened?"

Cass reached into the refrigerator and grabbed two bottles of Dunkel, setting one at the edge of Michael's plate and the other at the edge of her own.

"That bad?"

"Depends on how you look at it. Eat. How was work? How was class?"

Michael could have burst hating to have to wait for what he knew would be something he wasn't expecting. Possibly something he absolutely didn't want to hear. Instead, he played along.

"Work was wonderful. Class was, well....I could have done better. I just have so much on my mind, and you are not making it any easier on me right now."

"I know. I'm sorry. It's just the only way I know." She grabbed her phone from the counter behind her. "Here, I got this just as I was leaving for work this morning."

It was the email. That email. That one email worth opening.

Subject: RE: Master's Program Application

**Cassandra Miller,**

Thank you for your application to our Social Work Program. We would like to extend our congratulations as you have been accepted to the program with full tuition reimbursement with corresponding University employment. Please see attached job description and class schedule. Your enrollment must be completed by March 1st to secure your place in this program beginning August 12th.

Sincerely,

Erika Cooper

Michael was silent. He looked up from the phone to share his genuine feelings, a growing smile and the kind of eye contact that can speak a million words in a single silent second. He opened each attachment, scanning the information in between bites of steak and sips of Dunkel.

"I want to take it Michael. I've struggled with this ever since I got the bachelors."

"I know babe, me too."

"I never pushed going back because I knew if I had to pay for grad school, I would have to take a job I would probably hate just to pay off the loans. I want to help people, not work in some H.R. department or something. But that's what I would have had to do. I didn't tell you I applied for this because I didn't think I had a chance to get it."

"If you would have told me, I would have ensured you that you had a really good chance." He set the phone down, "and obviously you did."

"What do you think?"

"I support you. I think you would be crazy to turn it down."

"I'll have to quit working. I don't think I can do a full-time job and grad school on top of another part time job even."

"Of course. This is a once in a lifetime opportunity! Grab another couple of those beers, we need to celebrate!"

"I can take on another part time job between now and next fall. We can save up, buy the transmission, you know. We can stay here another year. We can wait on wedding planning. I don't want this to get in the way of your degree."

Michael scraped the last bit of egg noodles onto his fork. "My dad always said, 'You'll know when you know,' this is one of those moments Cass. Come on, let's walk to the park and get some snow shots."

---

Lewis was late. 7:07 a.m. He burst through the door straight to the order counter.

"Good morning, Lewis!"

"Michael, is it true? I heard you took a full-time job in the caves."

"It's true. I'll still be here though at least a few evenings each week and a couple Saturdays a month."

"When's your last day?"

"Friday, I start first thing Monday morning."

"But what about school, what about Cass? What does she think of all of this?"

"I was luckily in my grace period with school. I'll still finish the degree. Just putting it off a year or so." He reached to his side to grab a to go cup and started making Lewis' usual. "As for Cass, she was upset at first, you know just worried that I was doing something I didn't want to do."

"But you do want to?"

"Yeah man. I, um, well...it's actually kind of stressful to try to be in control of everything all the time. This feels right. Like an adventure. That's what life is right? An adventure."

"I like that, Michael. Someday, I'm going to try it myself. Life as an adventure."

# 2

# February

*Entirely iced over, encapsulated in a deep warm blanket
of snow. The tree limbs, every blade of grass, capable of
experiencing the sunlight of day looked as if they were
made of glass. The gnomes huddled among a fire below
their crude branch home, the fairies flittering about
bringing berries and nuts they had hidden from summer's
prosperous days. This was far from the European life
their ancestors had told them of, though it was those
stories that kept them pushing forward. Who would have
thought that a choice of becoming a castaway would lead
to such a new and challenging life that even after 300
years, held every thread of culture from the day the
tagalongs left to this very day that they now hid their
existence in the New World on the other side of the
pond.*

Eliza's pen refused to emit a single swipe of ink.
Frozen. She rolled it between her hands, slipped it into
her coat and to the center of her warm breast. Even her
coffee had lost its last bit of warmth.

*Oliftz, the eldest of the, t  th*

It was pointless. Sort of. Eliza was satisfied. Her
daily inspiration had paid off and it would last all the way

back through the woods, across the field, down the hill, past the tiny carriage house and back into her warm cozy home. She trudged along imagining the deadened thorns filled with luscious blackberries, the thick twisting vines dripping in giant green and red grapes. She listened to each and every song of her feathered winter friends and spoke aloud to them "You bring me joy today, as you do every day!"

Back in her house she tossed a few split pieces of oak into the fireplace. The kettle hanging above the flames soon sent its steaming cue that the coffee was hot once again. Eliza, having her pen warmed and flowing, continued the story of the tagalongs she imagined living in her own woods.

Of course, she didn't believe they were actually there. She did wonder though. That is what writers do. They wonder, what if? Then, sit pen to paper with their own mind's ideas of the answer. Eliza was so good at doing this she had written two bestsellers. She didn't even seem to mind that they were twenty and twenty- three years old.

Their fame was almost accidental in the first place. Writing novels was almost a therapeutic respite from the technical grind of small-town journalism. If not for the striking young man in the print department, she probably would have never even shared the first book with a single soul.

She thought of him as she sipped her coffee and began looking for a way to incorporate his perfect teeth, his deep blue eyes, and kind soft hands into the description of a young strapping gnome. She laughed remembering she was supposed to hate him. Though she didn't.

As it turned out, having NOT published anything since the second-best seller, had made her so famous, iconic if you will, that Eliza changed her name, grew out her hair, dying it straight black and moved to the middle of the country.

She had no friends, hardly an acquaintance, and had convinced herself she liked it that way. She had her cats, dog, and a riding horse. She wrote every day. However, outside of a dozen or so poems, Eliza had not finished a single story since the day he left.

She lifted the framed cover of the March 1989 issue of *Literary Life*, the headline *What's next for Eliza Manning?* The picture below a twenty –five-year-old Eliza, shoulder length strawberry blonde hair, brightly flowered pants and an oversized blue sweater standing on the ocean view deck of her undisclosed Rhode Island Cape Cod. Standing beside her sporting his favorite white slacks and pale-yellow breezy button up, his hair mousy brown and just slightly long in the back, he...Eliza interrupted her own thoughts of reminiscence, "Dear Peter, she thought aloud, do we really look twenty-six years older?"

She held the picture up next to her face in front of the parlor room mirror. Her skin wasn't as full looking, maybe not quite as soft looking. Besides that, she really enjoyed seeing she hadn't changed much. She did miss him, she did wonder from time to time where he was, what he was doing, what he looked like. But most of all, why he left.

Her friends all had their own ideas, mostly that her fame was too much for him. That her success diminished his manhood, he should have been the bread winner- not her. Even her publisher weighed in warning her to copyright every written word not yet published, in fear he would steal her work.

He didn't publish anything. He essentially dropped off the face of the earth.

Her own mother, who had adored him up until the day Eliza told her he had gone, took the thought to her grave that he was an espionage criminal complete with an alias name. "My dear girl, you brought so much attention to yourself and him both that he had to go to Mexico, I'm sure of that."

Gnomes, misplaced gnomes. She missed summertime. She missed the ocean. She didn't really miss Peter, though she missed his encouragement. She certainly didn't need him to publish another book. Then again, another book could be a flop making her two top sellers lose their collection status. Worse yet, another book could be another hit, putting her right back in the place that brought her here. Here was safe, somewhere no one knew who she really was. Here, she was just the strange lady who frequented antique shops, the farmers market, and the front south corner window of the coffee shop.

"Come cat" she called to the long black-haired tom curled upon the hearth as she took her coffee to the kitchen. The cat ran alongside her brushing twice against her legs, then flopped to the floor stretching his body until settling into a cock-eyed twisted position only a cat can consider comfortable.

Eliza pulled a notebook from a tidy stack on the kitchen table.

*Butter, potatoes, cheese, carrots-* a grocery list began to fill a half empty page previously occupied by a half-written poem. This was often the case with her notebooks. Every room of the house had tidy stacks of notebooks. Some labeled, most just partially written in, awaiting a possible return of Eliza's pen to complete the thoughts within them.

She daydreamed of summer, of her gardens and fresh tomatoes. Only the indoor portion of the farmers market was open. No local food until mid-May.

"Well cat, I suppose it looks like a good day for an outing. What do you say"?

His slight "mew" and tail tapping were sufficient.

The sound of her clunky keys being lifted off the hook at the front door stirred the sleeping cocker spaniel from her place at the hearth. "Oh, not today, Daisy, going to town."

Town was less than a mile from the house, though the old wood-grain AMC Eagle made its way as if on autopilot through the windy country road into a square of two-story brick buildings still somewhat unchanged from their 1800's beginnings. As Eliza neared the coffee shop her mind convinced her to park the car. She really didn't want a cup of coffee, though she did bring the notebook from her early morning writing time. Slipping the clip of the pen into the rings of the notebook she made her way toward the warm, inviting café.

It was busy, people going in and going out. She wondered if her seat at the window was open. To be sure she walked past the door to peek into the window. Sure enough, someone had taken it. A young man, probably early twenties with a stack of books and a small laptop sat punching away at the keyboard seemingly disconnected from the world inside and out.

Eliza kept walking. Down the street, across the street, up the street again. Her thick black boots took her straight to the antique shop. She enjoyed the sound of the bells crashing against the heavy glass door as she entered. The friendly shop owner called out to her by name, "Good morning, Jane! Haven't seen you in a while."

Eliza smiled, "Good morning to you Charlene." She really had no reason for choosing the name *Jane*, she just liked the sound of it.

"I got a bunch of new stuff in last week from an estate sale up in Henry County. It's in the back room." Charlene was always finding interesting items at estate sales from all over Missouri. Eliza enjoyed visiting with her. She had a story for everything in the store. Charlene had once even invited her to join her on a trip to a sale in Lafayette County. Eliza quickly dreamed up a reason to be out of town that day.

Though Eliza had nearly memorized every item in the store, the back room still mesmerized her. Clocks, framed prints, books, trinkets, and knick-knacks all filled the room from the floor to just feet of the ceiling and on tables and shelves. Eliza expected Charlene to join her

39

with the stories of the impressive items, however the bells of the door rang taking her to help other customers. Eliza didn't mind, she was getting anxious to get to the farmers market and back home.  A small blue ceramic elephant caught her eye as she started back toward the front of the store. The top of the elephant's back opened up to reveal the perfect place to keep tiny things like paper clips and push pins.  The price tag taped to its belly read $3.50. She was sold.

As she approached the counter, Charlene left the perusing couple promising to be right back.

"I love this little guy" she stated pulling the tag off the elephant. "Came from a yard sale just a few blocks away last summer."

As Eliza counted out the money from her bag, she could hear the couple getting closer, they were discussing a lamp they had picked up and how old it might be. The man said, "look at the base, see how it...." The woman interrupted him in a whisper loud enough for Eliza to hear.

"Honey look, that lady"

Eliza could feel her getting even closer. She could feel her staring. The woman continued, "I swear that's Eliza Manning."

Eliza grabbed the little elephant, "No need for wrapping. Just realized I'm running late for an appointment." She moved as quickly as she could without seeming to run, keeping her face away from sight as her eyes began to well. Steadfast past the glass cases of costume jewelry, steadfast cornering the display items at the front window, steadfast through the heavy glass door.

Straight to the car. Straight home.

_____

The elephant fit perfectly on the end table next to her favorite chair beside the hearth which was once again peacefully occupied by a lazy cat and a happy dog. Eliza pulled the grocery list from her pocket and picked up the phone.

"Yes, Jane Douglas 220 S. Pine Street. Five pounds of red potatoes, a large bag of carrots, two blocks

41

of sharp cheddar, two pounds of salted butter and tomatoes. Three, I guess. Just so long as they are red. I'll be home all day. Yes. Thank you."

*Oliftz, the eldest of the gnomes had requested a meeting with Thenarn, a young emerging leader among all misplaced gnomes. Thenarn took his seat at the Walnut stump table as many had before. Oliftz greeted him with the centuries-old rise, bow, and words of celebration, "For the joy of friendship"*

*Thenarn rose, straightened his pale-yellow shirt, bowed, then proclaimed, "For the love of summertime."*

# 3

# March

It was one of those days. One of those beautiful spring days. The kind that could convince you to drive past the high school your senior year and keep going. The kind that made you feel more alive than you had in months. One of those days that you notice everything. The yellow glow to the honeybee covered willow trees, the slight greening of the grass and clover, the blooming daffodils on the rising edges from roads to yards. Clara had hours before she had to be anywhere. Traffic was so light that she slowed the car to 30 miles per hour. Besides, there was no one behind her.

The light turned green. The clicking sound of the turn signal stopped as the car made a full right onto the highway. So many sights she hadn't seen since winter, or at least since the past November. Just as the leaves of the maple trees were slowly emerging from their tiny red buds, people were slowly emerging from the insides of their homes and businesses. Even the grocery store had filled the outside of its entrance with plants, flats upon flats of pansies. She laughed, every year the pansies come out when spring feels like it's set in stone and every year it's guaranteed that once the pansies come out there will be at least one more freeze. Poor pretty purple, red, and pink petals. There was more though, not just the early risers to bloom and replace the grey with nature's glorious color pallet, but every other form of nature seemed to have awakened as well. A groundhog scampered along the edge of the highway, a flock of robins prepping for spring nests and humans...humans out walking along the sidewalk going who knows where but out in the sun for that free dose of vitamin D so desired by all.

She parked the car. First stop a cup of coffee to refill her nearly emptied stainless-steel mug. She walked knowing the heavenly perfection of cool enough for coffee but warm enough for walking only comes twice a year. As she walked from the coffee shop toward the bakery, she celebrated the warmth of the sun soaking into her skin. The grassy spots between the tall brick buildings and the road's edges had taken on the neon hue of early green. Lunch for two, the first warm day of spring at Wagon Wheel Park, a tradition that felt as comforting and permanently secure in the same way her childhood church felt. As far back as Clara could remember, her mother would watch the weather forecast in anticipation of their *Welcome Spring Lunch*. Sometimes it would be as early as late February and sometimes as late as early April. It always consisted of two paper lunch bags and hours of fun on the swings, slides, and the seesaw. Clara felt a little badly about not making the lunch herself as she walked into the bakery, though she knew her mother would understand. Spring break was a vacation for the kids, for her it was catching up on grading papers, writing IEP reports, and finalizing lesson plans.

With two warm paper bags tucked into her backpack and the still steaming coffee she continued on through the last commercial block, into the region of transition where homes meet offices and offices meet municipal buildings only to return once again to homes of nearly every era of the modern story to the recent past. A small, faded plaque was all that remained of those who dwelt there before any houses were built. Clara didn't need the plaques that weren't there to explain why even most of those homes were soon lost to war. She didn't need the plaques that weren't there to explain why the homes that came after them were lost to *progress.* She didn't need the plaques that weren't there to explain why the old Five and Dime that provided her with an entire childhood of craft supplies sat empty and mothballed with its windows boarded and awnings removed. She imagined herself in her future classroom, explaining why places and things become neglected, how the once beloved could so quickly become a distant memory and sometimes forgotten completely. She imagined teaching these things to students old enough to understand. Clara didn't read the faded plaque, the one visible annotation that denoted evidence of an evolving story to reach the present day. She had memorized it years before, the day she walked to Wagon Wheel Park with her *Welcome Spring Lunch* announcement that she wanted to become a teacher. It was that plaque that set concrete to her decision, and once again it solidified the next step in Clara's journey of life.

---

He slowly meandered along the broken bits of concrete slabs that once made a perfect sidewalk for bicycle-led newspaper deliveries, large metal strollers and curbside metal framed woven lawn chairs for parades and block parties. Back and forth, back and forth, from the red architecturally lost fourplex that served a single family when the sidewalk had lay yet even. Back and forth while the cars passed by. While the old man drug his trash can to the curb. While the lady in pajamas took to the porch for a cigarette all the while carrying on with whoever listened on the other end of her phone.

No one stopped. No one came out of the red house, but the sun was warm, and it had been so long since he had felt that. He had spent so many days out in the cold, smashing his body below a warm truck or at least beneath the overhang of the shed behind the red house. It felt good to be warm, but it meant nothing compared to being loved.

47

She came walking by, not looking for anything. Just walking with an obvious destination. Just her backpack and two paper sacks.


Many did. Most crossed the street to avoid him. Some almost acknowledged him. None knew him, even the neighbors he did know seemed to pretend he wasn't there. But she stopped. She looked him in his eyes with something he had almost considered impossible. She had compassion.


"Hey buddy." She stooped to the ground. She wasn't who he was looking for. He knew they were gone, but it was his nature you see- his purpose to uphold his honor as the most loyal friend anyone can ever have. Ah, but the compassion...and French fries.


Clara continued through the uninterrupted land of neighborhoods. It saddened her to see they were not quite as beloved as her own childhood stomping grounds only a few miles away. The homes still held some resemblance to her early memories, though less and less bore the pride of ownership. Instead of *For Sale* signs, there were *For Rent* signs, many boasting a one- or two-bedroom unit. Then, the house with its inside furniture outside, and another with windows cracked and gutters sagging. Still, it was quiet. An occasional passing car, a bird, the sound of a trash can being dragged across the concrete, a woman chattering on her phone and a distant siren heading for who knows where. The whine of a dog. An old yellow, something. He meandered with a mission. Back and forth from one end of the block to the other. Back to a red fourplex bearing a *For Rent* sign. To the porch, to the right side and to the left. Then once again, block end to block end. She couldn't help it, he had so much love to give and no one to return the gift. "Hey buddy, hey." And soon, Clara entered the park with the large paper sacks filled with sandwiches, a few French fries, and an old yellow dog.

---

Clara found Emma sitting under a large white barked Sycamore tree holding her hand over her phone, likely looking at the app that showed where Clara was.

"Sorry I'm late mom, lost track of time."

"No problem, I could see you were close." Clara handed her the sack, "Skimpy on the French fries?"

"No, I...um."

"Ahh, I see you made a friend. What's his name?"

"Jacque!"

"Because he likes French fries?"

"Precisely."

"I'll bet he likes bacon too. There's just something about cold bacon I never could like."

"Pigs are smart mom."

"I know. I'm sorry, but Jacque will enjoy it right?"

And indeed, he did. He patiently kept nearby for any and every bit of whatever they were willing to share. He went along for the walk that followed the emptying of the sacks which Clara tucked into the front pocket of her backpack. She addressed Jacque as a human, "No grease Jacque, these get recycled." The old yellow dog turned his head cock-eyed with intense attention then perked his ears hearing the distant sound of laughing children. "You have enough time to sit at the playground a bit?" Clara asked Emma with a voice of expectation. She remembered the disappointment her mother felt when in sixth grade she suggested they watch the children play because she was too old for the playground.

"Of course, it's *Welcome Spring Lunch* tradition. I don't have to be back to the hospital until 1:30 for a staff meeting." Emma called to Jacque as they continued walking along the winding concrete path toward the overpass.

Clara stopped, "Mom, is that?"

"Yeah, it is. A homeless camp. There are several now. Wherever there's a patch of trees, an alley or anything resembling a place no one bothers. This one cropped up after our old hospital closed." She looked back at the old, repurposed building that she worked in for over twenty years. The building she said her final goodbye to her grandfather in and said her first hello to Clara in. She wondered how many of the people living in the makeshift tents wouldn't be there if they could be seen by the doctors and psychiatrists that the old building housed. "Some of my coworkers call them vagrants. As if they're rats or mice."

"Even rats and mice have their place."

"I know hon. I know."

The playground wasn't nearly as busy as they had expected. Clara didn't recognize any of the children. She loved seeing her students, though for this day she was glad to be outside in a different district than her own. "Quite a few of my students are out of town for spring break this week." She orated her thoughts to provide a possible explanation to the half empty swings and stationary seesaw. Emma squinted her eyes, "You sure they aren't all home playing video games?"

Clara laughed, "Of course they aren't, if they're home I'm positive they're wrapped up in a classic, you know like *To Kill a Mockingbird* or *Raisin in the Sun*."

Emma rubbed her hand over Clara's head, "Still my optimist. Speaking of which, did you get my email about the 3rd grade teacher opening? Just imagine teaching at the same school you went to!"

Clara dropped her eyes, "Yeah, I uh, I don't know mom. I really think I would enjoy teaching older students, maybe junior high."

"The worst years of human life. Just beginning to realize their passions and at the same time hit with having to figure out how to fit in."

"I know, that's part of the reason I want to teach that age. I haven't forgotten those years, and I think having someone slightly compassionate might help them lean a little more into those passions and a little less into buying into the idea that the social order of junior high will matter past junior high. Speaking of society, you and Lewis ever get together with friends? You know, dinner or anything?

"We visit with the neighbors. Barbeque season will be here before you know it. We're fine hon." She took Clara's hand, "We have you. Not all the time but maybe soon."

Clara didn't respond. She just stared at Jacque lying on the ground beside them, his front paws crossed, and back legs stretched out on top of his long scraggly tail. "You and Lewis mentioned retiring last weekend at dinner. I meant to ask what you guys are thinking about with that before we got on the subject of, gosh, what was it?"

Emma blurted her response, "Kentucky Blue Grass versus Fescue! Ugh, as long as it's mowed, I really don't care."

"That's right," Clara giggled, "I was trying to sway him to Buffalo Grass! Don't have to mow it as often.

Well, anyway, so out with it! I'm sure you two have at least talked about retirement plans."

"Well," Emma pressed her hands across her legs over her shiny purple scrubs. "A little. It's a fairly recent conversation. We talked about maybe doing a little traveling. When Lewis was a kid, his family went camping once in Hot Springs National Park in Arkansas. He thought it might be nice to take a trip every summer to a different park. Maybe drive and take as long as we want to get there, see some sights along the way. Lewis says it would be like living life like an adventure." She sounded happy sharing the possibility, each word sounding almost dreamlike. "But, I mean, that's a few years off Clara, and besides if you come back here to teach, we wouldn't want to be away from you for months at a time. Don't you worry about us!"

---

Emma offered to drive her back to her car. She refused. *How often do you get to see your own town at 3 miles per hour?*

She went north. Through the neighborhoods she rarely saw. "Jacque, doesn't it break your heart?" The old yellow dog responded with enough of a tail wag that he

became a friend for the purpose of thinking out loud. "All the trash! All the water bottles and aluminum cans-you realize 90% of this could be recycled. Worse than that, how did it get here? We're unconscious, you know that? Of course, you do." She picked up a large soda bottle, "Someone did the same to you as they did to this roadside. I'm sorry Jacque. I know your value, I promise."

---

Clara cooked because she enjoyed cooking. She especially liked to cook when she came home knowing the alternative would be something Emma had purchased in the frozen section of the store. With her phone connected to the stereo set on the *Iron and Wine* station she bustled around the small kitchen chopping veggies, checking a pot of quinoa, and stirring a pan of burger for Jacque.

The radio stopped as a call came in.

"Hey Zach. I'm leaving tomorrow afternoon. Really? I haven't seen her in years! No, it's no problem, the coffee shop? I can be there in 45."

Emma drug herself through the front door. "Clara?" No response.

Then, there in the dining room two plate settings, wine glasses, a bottle of wine, her large skillet covered, and a note.

She knew. She cried, but she knew before she was born. Clara didn't belong to her any more than anyone owns a beautiful sunrise even though she felt like an extension of Emma's own being.

Mom,

Went out to see some friends from High School. I made you dinner, it's in the skillet. I signed a four-year contract, got 9th grade history! We'll talk about it when I get home. I'm sorry I didn't tell you right away. I know it hurts, I hurt too. I promise to come home as often as I can, you can come see me every weekend if you want. Jacque's in the back yard. He's different from you and me mom. You loved me and I loved you back. Poor Jacque will love anyone without anything in return, I'm sure one of us can love him back like he deserves. Just imagine if we

loved everything and everyone as much as we love each other.

It'll be okay mom.

I promise.

P.S. Jacque told me he's never been to the Grand Canyon

Clara

# 4
# April

Andy busted through the front door of Annabelle's Garden Shop in his typical urgent steed. "Annabelle, hey, you in the back?"

A kind voice replied, "Yes Andy, I'll be out in just a second."

Andy helped himself to a glass of cucumber mint water from the end of the checkout counter, grabbed a catalog from the display below and made himself as comfortable as he could get at a small white wrought iron bistro table tucked into a corner surrounded by large ceramic pots filled with tropical hibiscus trees and bright green pouring ivy. Annabelle emerged from the back carrying a giant bouquet half as big as herself toward the front counter. She let out a loud sigh as she slipped it onto the glass countertop.

"Wedding bouquet?" Andy asked as his right leg bounced above his left.

"Yep, they'll be here to pick it up in about half an hour."

"Well good, then you can make the banquet."

She wiped her hands on her dirt covered apron and joined him at the table. "Yes, I'll be there."

"You don't sound overly thrilled about it."

"It's a love-hate thing Andy. I love seeing everyone, I hate the pomp and circumstance of these things. You'll be there, right?"

"Oh yes, and Frank." He put his hand to the side of his face as if to tell a secret then in a low whisper explained, "I promised him there would be Pinot Noir."

"And will there be?"

"I hope so, but just in case I have bottle in the car! Is Jordan coming?"

"Afraid not, he's working late today. How we keep the shop open."

"I know, I'm sorry. Speaking of which, did you hear?"


*Did you hear?* could refer to almost anything from Andy. He was the source of all downtown knowledge. The week before was the news that new streetlights would be going in around June. The week before that was that a couple new to town from Maine were looking into the empty building on the corner for a possible Irish Pub.

"I never hear anything from anyone but you Andy. Is the Irish Pub going to happen?"

"Oh, I don't know about that yet. That guy is waiting on restoration bids before he makes an offer. No, I'm talking about the bakery. They're closing next week."

"No!" Her hand hit the table, "Dammit, I thought they were doing okay. I mean they aren't packed all the time, but they have customers...happy customers, including me!"

"I know sweetie, I'm devastated. They didn't have any capital and had so many surprises."

"Like what? I mean I get it, anything involving food is high overhead, but they seem to have kept that streamlined."

"Well, first of all the music extortionists threatened to sue them even though they made sure they only played copyright free music."

"All three firms? On what grounds?"

"All three and on the grounds that they had a local musician play for their grand opening last summer. The letters from the lawyers stated that live music often includes copywritten songs."

"Okay if he did, I get it, but he didn't, I mean I don't think he did. Jordan and I were there that night. He announced each song as an original and I had never heard any of them before."

"Doesn't matter, these guys always win. It wasn't just that though, you know as well as I do that living the *American Dream* and owning your own business means taking the hardest hits. Tax incentives are for big corporations, big box stores and giant chain businesses."

Annabelle shook her head and rolled her eyes. "I wish I could help them. They were an anchor."

Andy drank the last of the water in his glass, "Me too, believe me. Losing them isn't just about losing friends, it'll cost us all."

---

The vintage wall clock above the "New Items" table rang five times. Annabelle had left a message and sent an email to the bride to-be. Now she would have to wait. She could clean, she could sweep the floors or dust nearly everything, she simply wasn't feeling it. She went back to the little white table and sat. She thought about the bakery, she thought about the clothing boutique that lasted eight months, the herb and spice store that made it almost a year before plastering its windows with *HALF OFF EVERYTHING.*

Andy had left the catalog on the table opened to the Anniversary section. Every November she carried his bouquet over to the coffee shop. He had been talking about this year's secret celebration since the day after last year's delivery. She already knew it would be the shiny 50$^{th}$ bouquet filled with silvery lilies, cream-colored roses, and white carnations. She stared at the bouquet on the counter she had so carefully arranged with gardenias, pale pink sweet peas, and reddish-purple orchids. She walked over to the cooler and pulled out one tiny white carnation, hiding it into the center of the bouquet. She whispered her secret wish, "May you have a vase full of these in 50 years." She imagined the future Mrs. Valdez's bouquet dropped across the head table of the reception as all the guests poured into the hall to eat a meal made by the restaurant across the street. She imagined the centerpieces being crafted by the Bridal Shop two blocks south. She imagined the caterer, the bar tender and the seamstress all getting to their homes at the end of the day, tired and exhausted but happy because they did what they loved. She imagined them taking their profits and showing up at the bakery to buy lunch on a Tuesday only to find that it was no longer there.

She knew a better way. But better ways are always the hardest to swallow. They take time, patience, creativity, and a giant dose of reality.

The familiar ding of the front door softly called her attention. A young woman in sweatpants and a tank top that read "Future Mrs." slowly made her way to the counter. "Are we feeling good?" Annabelle asked as the bride stared at the mass of flowers petting the petals of one of the gardenias. "Oh, yes, I'm actually feeling calm. I'm going to try to stay this way." She laughed as she handed Annabelle her bank card. "Good luck and I would love to see some pictures!" The bride gathered her flowers into her arms, "I'll post them when they come in and tag you! Thank you, Annabelle!"

Lights off, front door locked, open sign turned to *closed,* register locked, thermostat set to 76*, apron hung, alarm set. Annabelle walked out into the cool evening air into the alley lined with faded, popped and concrete-covered portions of brick. Her car sat warmed by the setting evening sun next to the giant landfill bin with one half of its rubber top flipped and the recycle bin with broken down boxes overflowing onto the ground. She stopped the car at an empty lot, *perennials*, she thought, mums and natives, spring bulbs, maybe a Japanese Maple. She took a deep breath and smiled as she let the image go into that place reserved for wishes that may never come true.

The speeches echoed throughout the wide square room while box fans hummed along the edges. Simple portable tables with black cloths and matching folding chair covers held everybody that arrived early. The rest stood in the breath of the fans.

Annabelle felt uneasy in her seat. She stirred, sipped her beer from the restaurant upstairs while fixating on those with no-where to sit. She wondered if anyone ate the orange gelatin. She hated potlucks. Her twenty years in Missouri had inundated her with them, in the previous twenty years of her life she had only been to two potlucks, one at a town hall wedding the other at a family reunion in her hometown's park. Orange gelatin, mandarin oranges, and whipped cream- it was the only *potluck* thing she felt she could do. Andy and Frank kept the conversations whirling during each break in speeches, all the while the warm bottle of pinot noir slowly drained from the table. Everyone became silent once again as the president of the Downtown Merchant's Group took to the podium.

"Okay everyone, time to get out your phones and check your silent auction bids, we have ten minutes left and counting before the live auction begins. And to speak of how important tonight's auction is I'll ask our Placemaking Committee Chair Annabelle Harris to tell you a little about where all this money is going!"

Annabelle reluctantly stood from her chair, smoothed out her long Aztec patterned skirt and tugged her brown knit blouse causing the wooden beads on her necklace to shift and sing as she walked toward the microphone. The president advanced the PowerPoint to the next slide to display a colorful hand drawn picture of a bench on the infill lot that was once occupied by a grand two-story Italianate shop until one day the wind blew too hard and proved that even the slightest neglect of bracing brackets can bring down a ton of bricks in an instant.

"After the loss of the bank then the dress shop two years ago, we decided that the best thing we could do is create opportunity..." she stumbled, "What I'm trying to say is that having an empty lot that we take turns mowing could be turned into a place for our customers to..."

Andy knew. He smiled and raised his glass toward her. She could hear his voice saying, *you can do this.*"

"Look, a couple benches, some flowers and some of those Edison style lights hanging from the two buildings left on either side would be a nice place for any of our customers to spend some leisure time." She paused again to see if he was still with her. He was and this time the smile had turned to a serious lip turned in and locked sort of way to beg her to say what needed to be said. She took a deep breath, "If we don't keep good strong businesses in our downtown districts, we won't have customers to sit on our benches." She pulled the microphone from the stand and walked toward the tables, "My husband isn't here tonight because he works two jobs to keep the shop open while we wish for the day it becomes profitable, and he can quit the second job." She walked up to Charlene, the owner of the Antique Shop and handed her the mike, "Tell them how you stay in business." Charlene's cheeks reddened a little as she stood up, "I sold my house and moved in with my dad. Last year I actually made a profit, but I know that until I hit three years in a row, I can't take chances. So, for now, I work at the shop six days a week and take care of dad on evenings and weekends."

"Thank you, Charlene." She walked toward Andy, he jumped from his chair and shared, "Same as Charlene as far as a year of profit, same as far as knowing better than to count on it just yet. Frank's company relocated to Springfield six months ago. He could have retired last year, but instead he sleeps on his son's couch Monday through Friday. We're dedicated to our little bookstore, but it takes years to convince book buyers that our store is a better value than saving a few bucks on a book shipped in a happy box."

Annabelle walked back to the podium, "Most of us have a similar story. There's nothing more difficult than trying to be in business for yourself. Most of us live week to week, hoping to still be in business the next. We can get a bench, and flowers and lights at any point. What we really need is a strong downtown. So, for tonight's auction, I propose we take every penny we bring in and create an interest-free loan program to keep our businesses in business and help get new amazing businesses started!"

An older man from the center of the room raised his hand, "I own the new gift shop on Oak. I did my research before starting my business to make sure I had the kind of products that would sell. How do we make sure we aren't giving a loan to a bad business that won't be able to pay us back?"

Andy ran to the podium, "Remember we're a Main Street community, we have tools and classes and people to help us make sure we're only financing businesses that have a really good chance of making it. They do all the data work for us."

Annabelle, laughed, "Thank you Andy. He's right everyone, they even helped me get started. Originally my business plan was focused on providing flowers for anniversaries and Valentine's Day until Main Street showed me most of those flowers are bought at grocery stores and gas stations. Instead, we focused on providing specialty flowers and seasonal items. We still have anniversary and Valentine's Day specials but in the last three years we've only sold just over a dozen total."

The president returned and advanced the next slide to show the auction goal created for the placemaking bench plan, $6,500. "Well friends, that amount of money could cover rent for several months, buy a needed piece of equipment, or help keep staff paid while a business grows to become self-sustainable. Someone get our secretary a piece of paper and a pen!" Annabelle pulled a notebook from her purse complete with a pen hanging inside the wire binding and ran it over to him. He then called to the board members for a motion, the owner of the gift shop complied, "I motion that this year's auction funds be used for the purpose of providing interest free loans to strong established and potential businesses to be paid in full in the course of 18 months." This was quickly followed by a "second" from the back of the room.

"Any discussion?" Three silent seconds passed, "All in favor?" A chorus of *Aye's* filtered toward the podium. "All opposed?" Another three seconds of silence. "Motion passed, let the bidding begin!"

The sounds of the auction began to fade as Annabelle slipped through the first door she could find in search of more chairs. "Do I hear $75? $80! $85?"

---

Annabelle was awestruck. She had found her way into the basement of one of the oldest buildings in town. A dimly lit, long, wide stone corridor lay ahead of her almost entirely untouched by time. She ran her hand along the sand-colored walls feeling the inconsistency of rock she assumed came straight from the earth, untouched by sandpaper or chisel. As she walked along, she came across wide wood framed rooms along the left side. She peeked inside each one, boxes, shelves, buckets but no chairs.

"It was a fruit market."

The voice startled her. "Andy! You scared me."

He laughed, "Sorry, I saw you slip out. Just wanted to make sure you were okay. You did a great job Annabelle! I'm proud of you!"

Andy caught up with her. "Thanks Andy. My heart's still pounding a little, but dang, I feel really good about this. So, fruit market, eh?"

They continued walking together, "Yep, over half the buildings here were grocers. That's how it was before A&P showed up. You got your fruit here, your bread down the street, your meat across the street and everyone had competition."

"Why did A&P change that?"

"They put everything in one store, fruit, meat, and bread. They bought it in bulk and often canned. They didn't deliver like the grocers did, you had to go get your groceries, pay for them, and take them home. They stocked their shelves for a fraction of the cost the grocers charged and had less staff...."

"Ah, so the groceries were half as much."

"Yep. The business owners fought it. Some states even made laws preventing A&P from buying in bulk, but in the end the grocers went out of business. Everything evolves and changes, so we adapt and change with it."

They reached the end, a door to the alley. It was unlocked.

The only sound in the alley was the clip clop of horse hooves pulling the town carriage across nearby pavement. Annabelle gently sat on the edge of a parking curb, "There's a shift right now. People are tired of going to the same brown and tan buildings for cheap junk, people want meaning...even in their stuff."

Andy lifted his hands toward the buildings, "These have character, definition, they tell a story. We connect with our customers, we listen to them, we offer them things that are unique and thoughtful. It won't happen overnight, but I do believe you're right. The shift is here and it's kind of exciting to be a part of it. It's also about time for Charlene's Thomas Hart Benton original to come up for auction and if I don't get back in there Frank is going to wipe out this month's profits on it."

"You go ahead, I'll be there in just a few."

Annabelle walked along the alley until the pavement returned to the original brick road. The air had become cold with the setting of the sun and a slight breeze that passed by every few minutes. The clip clop of horse hooves got louder and louder as the carriage came closer to the brick road. Now she imagined the blacksmith turning out horseshoes and wagon axels, the farmer from the countryside bringing in barrels of wheat from the mill, the traders arriving from Santa Fe with mules which would in a few decades head west pulling a wagon train of hopeful homesteaders off to Oregon. She silently shook her head and smiled as she thought of the day the transcontinental railroad put an end to trail travel and every business that supported it. *Trains, Interstates, Big Box Stores, shopping malls, the internet....corporate welfare...adapt, adapt, adapt.*

She closed her eyes as the sound of horse and wagon once again faded away. In her mind's eye she conjured people, lots of people, laughing, eating their lunch on a sturdy iron bench. Children playing tag among pink and red azaleas. Herself, standing near the towering old brick wall beneath the sagging Edison lights, and of

course, flowing long branches filled with silk-like red leaves of a Japanese maple tree.

# 5
# May

Six a.m., not one, not two, but three alarms to be sure. One on the other side of the room, one on each phone.

The coffee pot, perking its last perk, filling the condominium with the strong welcoming aroma of Monday. The sun, beaming in through the east facing bedroom window, slightly cracked as the night before was unusually warm. A slight humid breeze poured past a blooming peony into the room. Coffee and peonies. A best-selling candle?

Mira smelled nothing, saw nothing, sensed nothing.

Austin smelled nothing, saw nothing, sensed nothing.

Mira stirred, haphazardly smacking the snooze on her phone. Haphazardly smacking Austin.

Austin startled and turned his alarm off. He exited the bed with a mission, hitting the alarm on the other side of the room. Straight to the shower.

Mira, not at the sound of a returned alarm, instead responding to the sound of emails and texts, app alerts coming through her phone- wrestling herself to the kitchen. To that perfect pot of coffee. To a mug, to the high-top kitchen table that she and Austin spent months picking out. To her laptop, scanning client emails and department store sales, her calendar. Her calendar...9 a.m. Allen Jones- New catering company. 10:30 a.m. Mildred Beck- Opening a tri-state burger franchise, eight locations. Noon, lunch with Strategic Solutions LLC, she smiled, and thought aloud, "Over 75 corporate offices each with their own cafeteria, I've been trying to get these guys to switch to us for over five years."

Austin joined her at the end of the table. His own laptop, his own check of emails and sales and calendar events. They could see each other's eyes just slightly peering over the screens.

"Five years huh? What made them change their mind?"

"They haven't yet, but they will. Pricing. Their costs just went up 12% which means going with us now will save them 7%."

"You get that one and we're celebrating!"

"Dinner at Petunia's?"

"Absolutely. Hey, speaking of plans, don't forget we're meeting that rep from Minos Co at four. After that we can head out to Petunia's for dinner."

"You seem pretty confident that I'll get that." Mira loved that Austin always believed in her. She wondered if he knew how many times his confidence in her was the only thing that got her through some of her toughest sales. She quickly switched back to her calendar from the *One Day Only Must Have Business Attire Sale.* "Four?"

"Yep, four on the dot. You know how farmers are."

"Okay, and no, *you* know how farmers are. I have a one o'clock conference call with corporate- it's the monthly call so I'll be on it for at least an hour and.....I have a two-thirty coffee with Isabell." Mira slid her phone into her hand from the edge of the counter, "I can cancel that."

"No, no. You never get to visit with her anymore. It's only a forty-minute drive. That at least gives you over half an hour to visit."

Mira reached her hand across the table and found his, "'Tis why I love you. You're right. I'll try to get through the conference call early, the last twenty minutes are always distribution updates, I can just put myself on mute and sneak out."

Austin sipped his coffee, lifted his glasses from his eyes and slowly dropped the screen halfway, "Then it's a date."

Jonathan was waiting in the lobby as Mira ran through the doors nearly twisting her ankle as her three-inch heels slid across the slick tile.

"Did you get it? Tell me you got it?" He begged as he tried catching up with her pace as she headed straight for the conference room.

"Of course, I did. We're late."

Jonathan blocked the door to the conference room, throwing his hand up into the air for the long-awaited high-five. "You rock Mira!"

"Is Austin taking you to Petunia's?"

"That's the plan! Let's get in here."

Ten chairs, eight filled. The voice coming from the speaker in the center of the table filled the room. Quietly, Mira and Jonathan took their seats. Jonathan mouthed the words "She got it," while pointing to Mira. Everyone made silent gestures of celebration.

*Profits are up 2% over last quarter, which is exactly on target, and our share prices closed at $67.85 yesterday, that's a temporary drop. Give it a couple weeks for the burger recall to be forgotten and we'll be back into the high 70's again.*

*Huston here, what burger recall?*

*Hey Huston, you guys are doing great out there! We'll cover the recall with supply disruptions.*

Mira flipped the packet of notes in front of her upside down, pulled a pen from her backpack and began writing. A few minutes later she held the note up for everyone to see:

Got a Two O Clock

I'll call in on my phone and

stay on the call until then

The air had become hot and muggy, *you never know what month May will feel like*, she thought to herself as she connected the conference call into her car stereo. All the way to the coffee shop the head of distribution listed one disruption after another.

*Freezes last autumn in Idaho caused potato crop failures, Wisconsin and Colorado fared much better but as supplies are dwindling our costs have gone up substantially. For this reason, we will be importing potatoes until this coming summer at the earliest. The ongoing droughts and fires in California have continued to reduce the supplies of wine, milk, and vegetables. Right now, however, we are on target to fill all vegetable orders from Arizona. The beef burger recall is currently only, I repeat only affecting our frozen pre-made patties and five-pound tubes. This is creating a one-to-two-week backlog from our regular suppliers. We have access to Brazilian beef but will only order if absolutely necessary. Do not advertise that to anyone.*

It was five after two. Mira carefully put her phone on silent and put it into the front pocket of her backpack. Isabell was patiently waiting at the first table on the right.

Isabell looked at her watch and laughed as Mira slipped into the seat next to her. "But we're actually having coffee Liz!"

"I'm having coffee. Are you getting anything?"

"Yeah, sorry. What a day!"

"Isn't every day."

"Touché"

Mira set the backpack on the floor next to her chair and made her way to the counter. "I'm celebrating a good day, Olivia. How about a Mocha Latte?"

The barista spun to her side to grab a mug, "Oh hey, we're out of soy, something about too much rain last year. You cool with coconut milk?"

"Yeah, that's right. I knew that. Coconut milk sounds great, probably a better choice anyways."

"It actually is, and I think it tastes better. That'll be four seventy-five."

Mira carefully carried her steaming cup of celebration java with a tulip design made of well-crafted mocha back to the table. "I'm here until three-twenty. How the heck are you?"

"I'm great Mira! The kids are great, Tom's great. Work is.... work, but anyways, what happens at three-twenty?"

"I have to leave to meet Austin at the farm. We have a meeting with a company that wants to lease the place this summer."

"For what? Have you guys looked into selling it?"

"To plant it. That's how farmers do things these days. Well, I guess farmers. It's a big corporation, so I guess they hire farmers? Anyways, Austin loves that place, he basically grew up there and it's so hard for him to think about selling it. But I really appreciate all your help with the deed transfer."

"Look Mira, I deal with this sort of thing all the time. It's not just that people become attached to their family property, it *represents* their family. That farm represents Austin's grandparents, give him all the time he needs."

"I am. Now seriously, back to you. Did Tom get the promotion?"

---

The afternoon sun poured into the car as she turned east toward the farm. A distant roar of thunder echoed through the cracked window. From her rearview mirror she could see a massive cloud moving toward her like a giant white shelf hovering over the earth. With each ever-loudening clap of thunder the cloud lit up in bright blue sparks like varicose veins across the sky. Soon the sun was gone as if someone had turned off the switch on daylight. The winds seemed to come from out of nowhere shaking the car as she held her foot on the break wishing the light would turn green.

Green. Go.

The song on the radio stopped.

The chilling sound of the emergency alert system going into action took over followed by a computerized voice from the National Weather Service. Before the word *tornado* could air, the loud sound of an alert blared from Mira's phone, only jarring her further. Being exactly halfway between the farm and her office she decided she might as well head for the farm. It was when the police cars began running up and down the highway with their sirens on that she decided to go straight for the large brick gas station half a mile ahead.

There were only a few cars in the parking lot. She hardly hit the brakes as she whipped the car left across the highway, past the pumps and into a front and center spot. Mira grabbed her purse with her right hand while opening the door with her left. She wasn't sure it had even shut as she hit the lock button on her key and ran to the door.

Locked.

The door on the east, locked. She ran back to the car.

The car door was locked. She was panicking. She hit the unlock button over and over. Jumped back in and put the car in reverse. The wheels squealed as she sped backwards, then forwards, back onto the highway as the sirens kept blaring on the radio, on the phone, and from the police cars. She prayed and thought of foxholes.

She sped. Just ten miles per hour over, it was foreign to her. But she sped. The light at the bridge turned red. A dark ominous green sky raced toward her. There wasn't another car within sight. *It was worth the ticket,* she thought. *They would understand,* she thought.

The rain became so heavy she could hardly see. Hail, wind, lightning. The car shook forcefully this time as if an earthquake had rattled the ground below her. She pulled over unable to see. She cried. Just two miles from the farm, just two miles from Austin.

She put her flashers on, *what does it matter*, she thought? Anyone could come behind her, they wouldn't even see her car. And then it stopped, it all stopped. She threw the car in drive as she recalled standing out in the field as a girl, hanging the clothes on the line as the lightning lit up the sky far in the distance. Her grandmother pulling the old wooden clip from the woven basket, the kind that doesn't bend, "If the storms come and then they suddenly stop, you'll know there's a tornado."

She turned the radio off. She turned the sound off the phone. The sirens were too far away to hear. All she could do was drive.

---

Austin was waiting for her on the front porch as she whipped across the muddy gravel driveway landing the car sideways on the small concrete slab that led to the sidewalk to the house.

"Mira, come on! Hurry!"

She bailed out of the car taking nothing with her. Austin grabbed her by the arm pulling her into the house, straight to the back and down the stairs to the basement. A small radio in the corner of the room screeched out three high pitched intermittent beeps followed by one long tone, *The National Weather Service in Pleasant Hill has issued a tornado warning for Northeast Jackson County and East Lafayette County until five twenty p.m. At three fifty p.m. doppler radar indicated a severe thunderstorm capable of producing a tornado near*

*Raytown moving Northeast at twenty miles per hour, the storm capable of producing a tornado will be near North Blue Springs by four twenty p.m., Buckner by four forty p.m., and Levasy by four fifty p.m. If you are in the path of this tornado seek shelter in a basement or inside an interior room....*

The radio went silent. They could hear the sound of hail beating down on the metal roof, a clap of thunder so intense they could feel the shaking of the house above them. Austin dug into his pocket to turn on the flashlight on his phone. "There's a box somewhere down here with candles and batteries, might even be a flashlight. Grandpa was really good about being prepared for anything."

The light from the phone was enough to find the old worn cardboard box with the faded words *Emergency Kit* handwritten on the front. Inside were two flashlights, half a dozen candles, a couple boxes of matches and an old coffee can full of batteries. Soon the room glowed as the tiny fires illuminated the white painted stones that made the basement walls.

Mira carried an old dining room chair from a back corner and pulled a big rocking chair up to the small table where the radio sat waiting for batteries. "I'll have it up and running in just a minute," Austin promised as he popped out the old batteries one by one matching the positive and negative ends to their proper places. "Got it!"

A moment of static filled the air as Austin gently turned the dial until a station came in .....*a tornado warning for North Central Lafayette County.....*

It was over.... for them at least.

"God, Austin, I was so scared. I didn't know what to do, where to go. I couldn't get into the gas station because the doors were locked. I didn't know if you were okay, I couldn't see the road, I.... I....."

These are the silent moments one questions being alive, the silent moments one tries to replay what just happened. The silent moments that reveal that everything that mattered doesn't anymore.

They held each other as they climbed back up the wood plank stairs and back outside to assess the damage. The wide-open fields that lay beyond the hundred-year-old family home revealed spring's neon green with each distant flash of lightning. Each clap of thunder echoed across the prairie sky with no way to tell just how far away the storm had gone.

A maple tree lay broken in half across the concrete slab, its top rested on the hood of Mira's car.

The yard was covered in debris, branches, shingles, bits of wood and twisted metal and yet the house survived completely intact outside of one broken window.

She couldn't help it. She laughed. Not the kind of laugh that occurs when someone hears a great joke. Not the kind of laugh that fills in the empty spaces of nervousness when words refuse to materialize. A rare kind of laughter, the kind that expresses shock and joy all at the same time, then quickly turns to an emotional explosion of tears and sobbing. They were alive, each secretly questioning that fact while embracing the seeming reality that they truly were not dead.

For one short moment the clouds thinned, allowing a slight bit of sun to pour out, and then it began to rain. Not a light rain, not a sideways rain, just straight down like the backside of a waterfall.

---

Austin had removed nothing from the house after his grandfather passed except for perishables in the refrigerator.

"It's not Petunia's cuisine, but I found a package of burger, a few jars of canned tomatoes and a can of chili beans." Mira carried the frozen red and white tube of meat labeled **BEEF** in her hands to a bowl in the kitchen sink. The spigot dripped out a small stream of water until it simply trickled and stopped.

"Ah the joys of country living," Austin laughed, "I'll go out to the barn and see if I can get the generator going. Well water doesn't flow without electricity."

"I guess you learn something new every day." Mira turned off the spigot and began searching for all the cooking implements she would use, just in case.

"Wait, what about the guy we were supposed to meet?"

"I almost forgot about that! I doubt he'll be coming out tonight. I'll call him though just in case."

"How, don't we have a signal?"


Austin smirked as he walked past her to the small round kitchen table, looked up the number on his cell phone and picked up the corded phone from the wall.

"You kept the land line active?"

"Out here, it can be your only lifeline to the world outside."


The Minos Co rep wasn't coming, no one was coming or going anywhere for a while. A tornado can

take out a house in an instant, but a heavy rain can flood out a highway for days.

---

Mira was up before the sun. She felt strange wearing Austin's grandmother's nightgown and robe, and yet honored at the same time. Quietly she made her way around the kitchen with a flashlight, pans under the cupboard to the right of the sink, wooden spoons in the drawer directly above. Mismatched plates, forks, and knives. She carefully lit the gas on the stove, setting the blue and white Corning Ware percolator above the flames. She stared at the calendar still turned to March and cried thinking about how much more time they could have spent with Austin's grandparents. How much time they spent growing their careers instead of living their lives. How unhappy Austin was in town, how much she actually hated her stupid three-inch heels. She silently laughed at herself as she recalled nearly buying even more heels, more suits, more things she didn't need and actually didn't even want, only twenty-four hours before.

"Smells good in here! What's for breakfast?" Austin sat down at the table as if Mira was about to serve him a cup of coffee along with the daily paper.

"Oatmeal and applesauce, and if we're still here tomorrow *you're* making breakfast." Mira set a cup, a spoon and two bowls in front of him before returning with the percolator, the pan of oatmeal and a mason jar of applesauce. He slowly poured his coffee into the little white mug with a thin band of tan near the top while staring at his empty phone. "You know honey," Mira explained as she scooped a spoonful of applesauce into her bowl, "staring at it won't make it work."

"Yeah, I guess you're right." He sat the phone down on the table and turned his attention to the oatmeal.

"Speaking of which though, I did make a quick call to Jonathan this morning to let him know I won't be in for at least a day or two. He said it really didn't matter, half the city is without power, and the trucks can't get in. Instead of buying more food from us, several of the restaurants and cafeterias are throwing food away, just like the ice storm in 02."

"Oh my gosh, I forgot to ask about the sale. You got it, didn't you?"

Mira pursed her lips and closed her eyes, "Yeah, put in a massive order for them yesterday, chicken from Iowa, tomatoes from a hot house in Wyoming, cheese from Wisconsin, frozen beef patties from Brazil..."

"Brazil?"

"Sorry, I'm not supposed to talk about that. Austin, what did your family grow here?"

Austin wanted to know more about Brazil but saw where she was going with the whole thing and moved on. "Well, before the war, I mean World War II, we pretty much grew everything. There's pictures around here somewhere of my great grandparents in the *kitchen garden*. Great grandma grew just about every vegetable under the sun AND canned enough to feed the whole family all year long. We had a couple milk cows, a few meat cows, chickens, and an orchard twice the size as it is today- apples, cherries, peaches, and pears. Every year they would trade a calf for a pig with the German family across the road."

"I do remember your grandpa talking about that."

"But for profits they mostly grew potatoes. They did sell extra eggs, milk, and cheese in town."

"Didn't they have a market stand on the highway?"

"My grandparents did, yes. My grandpa had four siblings growing up so they pretty much ate everything this farm could produce, but Grandma and Grandpa only had my dad to feed."

"What about after the war. When did it all change?" She could tell the question saddened him, but to her the answer to what happened to the Byrne family farm could explain the entire current food system.

"Um, you know it was gradual. Potatoes slowly lost their zeal as a cash crop, really for the reason we're stuck here right now. Flooding, unexpected freezes and hot spells are all bad for potatoes, well, you know that. Anyways, first corn and wheat took over, then it became today's rotation of corn and soybeans. The kitchen garden went from one acre to a half-acre to a small spot in the yard by the time I came along. Half of the orchard was cut down when my dad graduated from high school since he went to college instead of taking over the farm."

"Which is why he gave it to you."

"Mira, I don't really know if he just doesn't want to mess with it or if he hates the idea of someone else owning it outside of the family."

"I would guess it's a little bit of both. It just seems so ludicrous to have all of our food shipped in from all over the country when we could source it all right here. Not just this farm, all the farms. I HEARD COWS this morning. They're so close I can hear them, and yet we're getting beef from...."

Austin couldn't let it go, "Brazil."

"This way guys," Mira made an onward motion movement with her right arm as her rubber boots splashed across the small creek that ran alongside the orchard, "I really think you'll love this, Liz."

Isabell and Tom followed behind her, each with one child in tow.

"This will be the flower garden, almost two acres of zinnias, roses, lilies, and daisies. I already have orders from that florist a few doors down from the coffee shop. Come on, let's go back toward the house. I want to show you where we're putting the greenhouse and the chicken coop."

"I draw the line on chickens Mira." Isabell laughed while her toddler made his best attempt to crow like a rooster.

"You are contracts Liz, but if you're up to it we'll take all the manual labor we can get."

"*Where* are you getting laborers Mira?" Mira imagined Tom had already crunched the numbers in his accounting brain and saw no possibility the whole thing would work.

"That part is interesting Tom," Austin couldn't wait to answer. "Every Saturday will be a *Work and Take* day. People can come out to the farm and trade labor for food. It's actually not a new concept. I'm also remodeling the second floor of the barn into a small apartment, for a WWOOFER. There's this website where people go to find a farm to live on, they might want to come for a week or maybe even a year. It's sort of like having an intern, they get room and board, you get another hand on the farm. And then of course we'll have to have a few full-time employees for distribution and your lovely wife part-time to handle the contracts."

The afternoon sun poured across the long wide front porch as an invitation for everyone to kick back and enjoy what little remained of spring's temperate air. Isabell kicked off her boots and rested her feet atop the porch railing. "Have you contacted any other farmers yet?"

Mira picked up a hard-bound notebook from the small wicker table next to her with her own pencil sketched *Fifty Mile Distribution* logo on the front, "Ten out of twelve are interested. Some of them already sell directly to a few local restaurants and one school district, but they all said that if the contracts come in, they'll grow more food for us to sell."

"What did Jonathan say when you told him?"

"That I'm nuts, and it won't work, but to keep his number just in case it does. Liz, the condo is empty, Austin already has the website built and his dad turned over the farm account to us to fund everything. There's only one way to go from here.... forward."

"If you really make this happen, Mira, all those fields we passed on the way here could be filled with green beans, carrots......"

" *We* will make this happen Liz. And um.... tomatoes. You know, the little heirloom cherry tomatoes, red, yellow, and purple. Anything but soybeans!" She laughed knowing that scenario wasn't likely and at best would take decades. "Who knows, maybe we can convince congress to pay people to grow vegetables on those thousands of acres they normally get paid to grow nothing on." Mira set the notebook back down on the table and jumped to her feet. "One more thing you have to do Liz. Trust me, you'll never buy another strawberry from the store again after tasting one of these."

The two dreamers walked back across the field to a long narrow strip bursting with white flowers and a handful of green and bright red strawberries. The berry patch buzzed with nearly a dozen honeybees bouncing back and forth between the flowers. Their tiny pollen-packed legs hung from their bodies as they lifted up into the air. Like an unbalanced first-run helicopter, their clear wings carried them over the farm, across the road and through a patch of wrangled but very alive woods. Only three weeks since the tornado and already the land had begun to repair itself. The bee bundle emerged from the trees into a small field left alone just long enough that briars, ferns, and thistles had emerged from the scarred soil in anticipation of becoming a forest. One lonely cottonwood pierced the sky with arms outstretched in every direction. A fuzzy grey squirrel chattered from atop a north-reaching arm at a friendly, red-bellied woodpecker looking for his lunch in the center of the tree. The bees buzzed past them both into a small hole along a thick dead limb and quickly unpacked the pollen into a cell for future baby bee food. Future organic, chemical free, unmodified strawberry pollen baby bee food. All within five miles of the hive.

# 6

# June

The song of an energetic cardinal made its way all the way from a nearby weeping willow to Opal's opened windows. *Cheer, cheer, cheer*, he called as he flew out to a tall wide cedar. *Cheer, cheer, cheer* and back to the willow. Opal loved the free entertainment. She loved the time of year. Cool enough for open windows from sunset to sunrise and exceedingly warm enough to enjoy being outside all day. From the kitchen windows she could see the park, the squirrels scampering about, chatting about whatever it is that squirrels chatter about. She could see the moms, dads, and grandparents pushing toddlers on swings and catching them at the ends of the slides. She could see the tents off in the distance, deeper into the thick patch of trees. Some were made of cardboard, others from blankets and sheets hung from low hanging branches. She only imagined what their world was like. She imagined making it better.

From the other side of her big brick open room that served all the purposes of a home without so many walls she could see her little town waking up. Sitting on a high-top chair at her shelf-style plank desk she sipped her tea waiting for a blue Ford Focus to pull in and park in front of the bookstore. Out came the owner with an armload of books, his keys dangling from his finger. While he fumbled with the books to unlock the door, she could hear the owner of the neighboring business *call* out "Morning Andy." Soon after, she heard the slamming of heavy truck doors and distant murmurings of men. Bending her head to the north, she could see a small construction crew with orange hard hats making their way down the street. She remembered hearing something about new streetlights being installed. Everything began to open all at once while the patrons and workers steadily filled the empty parking spaces. A small commotion arose right below her as two older women were approached by a homeless woman asking for change. "Get away from us." one loudly retorted. "Go on, get out of here," the other added as they scrambled away from the benign request. Opal wanted to yell to them from her window, *yes, yes, back to the woods you go, how dare you come out of hiding!* She imagined the women holding their tithing up high for all to see from a Sunday pew, then telling their grandchildren at Sunday dinner how much they help the poor with their donations. She wondered if it ever occurred to anyone that there's a reason they end up there in the camps in the first place. If anyone ever considered the possibility that as a culture we have knowingly stood back and allowed this to happen. Opal thought about how every kindergartener is convinced they will someday have some incredible, *successful* career, live in a big house, have the latest greatest stuff. Maybe even a few kids or at least a designer dog. She opened the folder from her desk to a page titled, *Grant notes*, and began to write- *We're a culture that calls everyone who achieves societal success winners, and anyone who falls short....losers. Shunning our fellow human beings, let's be honest, our neighbors, is a failure of humanity itself."*

The courthouse clock tower rang nine times. Nine, one less than ten, which meant Opal had less than an hour to make her first appointment of the day. She picked up her phone to check the weather but before she got to the app an incoming call took over. "Anna! How are you? Yeah, I would really appreciate that. I can be there in fifteen or it'll have to be after lunch sometime." She pushed the sliding doors to her bedroom open, threw on the first articles of clothing she saw, grabbed the folder from her desk and ran down the stairs. Carmen, her one and only employee was waiting for her in the studio, "Opal, I got a call for a ten by seven print of Life Rock, I can't find one."

"Sorry, I'll call you later," and she ran out the back door to her car. She gently tossed the folder onto the passenger seat and leaving the door open, walked back toward the studio. She stopped at a small patch of grass between the building and the alleyway with nothing but a picnic table. A picnic table that no one had sat at for nearly a year. She imagined John Doe, alive and smiling. She clenched her jaw as the vision of the blanket-wrapped body lay slumped and motionless across the seat and top.

She recalled the impromptu prayer group that formed while everyone waited for the police to arrive. She recalled the silent promise she made to the pale young man as the EMT's loaded him into the ambulance. "I'm working on it, Mr. Doe, I'm working on it," she whispered to the wind.

---

Opal checked her watch for the third time in five minutes. She had met Anna many times, though always in the world of art. This would be a refreshing interview, something much bigger than exhibits and much deeper than delving into the mind of the creative. The picture perfect little white heart shape in her cappuccino had faded into a vision of abstract. She sipped the sweet, caffeinated nectar, took a deep breath, closed her eyes, exhaled, then eyes back opened. She wasn't nervous by any means, simply tight on time for the day. She peered over to the legal sized folder labeled, *Garden of Grace* which sat just next to the cappuccino on the small round table. Looking up, she was relieved to see Anna coming toward her.

If there had been a mythical architype of *classic*, Anna exemplified it. She stood about 5'6", grey pant suit, red bun, wire rimmed glasses and serious to the core. Her standard 4"x8" notebook barely rose out of the center of her long stranded basic black purse that hung without movement as she received the cardboard wrapped paper cup steaming with black coffee from the counter. Opal was essentially her *other.* Shorter, long face, high cheek bones, long dark braids and blunt bangs that fell along a nearly makeup free, though slightly suntanned face. Opal's airy white knit summer sweater hung above a pair of baggy tan cotton capris. Anna stepped toward the table with each press of her black pumps creating a slight click as they lightly tapped the hardwood floor. Opal met her in the middle, silenced by a pair of rope sandals. A seemingly odd friendship embraced by a genuine hug. Then again, when humans cease to care what other humans think, amazing things can happen.

Anna sat opposite of Opal tossing the notebook onto the table. "I take it we're still exclusive?" She asked with a slight laugh.

"Yes, indeed my friend. Never have and never will trust thy local broadcast of entertainment, I mean *news.*"

"You know, they aren't all entirely bad."

Opal smirked, "I prefer facts over Gotchas. Either way, there is something sacred to me about print."

"You still get our paper?"

"Every day. And on the rare occasion I don't like something I simply turn it to compost. That way everyone wins."

"Nice, Opal. I suppose I appreciate that. I know you have to get on to bigger things today, so we'll get started. Garden of Grace, right?"

"Yes. And it's official. The board approved the name last week."

"What inspired you to pursue this idea?"

"It was a combination of happenings, anything worth doing is." She sipped the slightly cloudy cappuccino, "To begin with, I was upset about the park development."

"Wagon Wheel Park?"

"I hated the idea of bringing a developer in for the sole purpose of pushing out the people we don't want to see. It's deeper than that; finding John Doe last summer, it still haunts me. Did you ever find anything out about him?" Anna shook her head no, "Sorry, he was probably a transient."

Opal pulled the day's newspaper from under her folder and read the headline Anna had typed just the night before, *Local Iraq war veteran found dead in car.*

Anna sighed, "It was officially declared a suicide this morning. It's not just here Opal, it's everywhere, every city, every town in America. I'm with you, but why the old plant? Some would say it's an unconventional way to use the property."

"I call it artistic adaptive reuse." Opal smiled a little, she was particularly proud of this. "I helped host an art competition several months ago. One of the submissions was a series of black and white photos of this old electronics factory titled *Ghosts of Manufacturing*. It deservedly earned several awards including being featured in *Through the Lens* magazine. Anna shook her head, "Ah yes, we printed something on that."

"I had no idea that plant was here Anna! They made Parker brand televisions, radios and even some appliances for over forty years. So, right there in front of the photographer, some guy announces, "It's a good thing you got those pictures when you did. You know they're gonna finally knock it down."

"He didn't."

"He did."

"That's when I started digging in. Went down to city hall to find out when it was slated for demolition. Of course, you know it wasn't yet."

"It's funny how if someone mentions something during a city council meeting it suddenly becomes a definite happening."

"Turns out some investor bought it ten years ago planning to turn it into a factory for manufacturing printers. Right after it was purchased, the company decided to move production to Japan."

"Japan? I can't imagine labor is that much cheaper there than here."

"It's not as cheap as other parts of Asia, but machines are and the maintenance that goes with them is highly available there. You know, I stopped in a fast-food restaurant the other day to use the bathroom and I noticed the soda machine's autofill. As in a cup falls down into place, it moves to a filling spot and the ice and soda pours in an exact amount. If labor isn't cheap, robotics are. That's something to think about. So yeah, the owner not only never did anything with it, but also stopped paying property taxes on it about five years ago. The city just acquired legal ownership a few months back, hence it being brought up at the city council meeting."

"That's right, I remember that now."

"I got an architect out there, we came up with a plan to use as much of the structure as we can, estimated total cost, grants, started the non-profit and bought it."

"When does construction start?"

"We'll start prepping next week. Have to make it safe for the workers. I've even got a work release crew, all non-violent convictions."

"You know you'll still get flack for that."

"Wait until they find out who will be living there. There's hardly any residential properties in the area and besides, from the work crews to the future residents there will always be supervision to keep everyone safe."

Anna checked her watch, "I'll have to get back to the office in half an hour. Can you give me a brief description of the end result?"

"Have you ever heard of a Poor Farm? They were common back in the day. We had one here, now it's the county hospital. They weren't perfect but I'm playing off that concept. We treat people in distress like plants, provide water, soil, and sunlight, however we could care less if they produce fruit. Fruit is plant purpose. What is human purpose? Everyone has something that brings them joy, it might be creativity like poetry or art, gardening, working with animals, cooking. Whatever it is, it has value and when people are provided with a setting for these ideas to flourish, there's a powerful healing affect." She could see she was going off course and realizing her time with Anna was waning, so she proposed her own non-corporate version of an elevator speech. "Imagine a safe place to live, small and simple but safe and comfortable. Common areas for dining and gathering. Like the Poor Farms, residents can work in the gardens to grow healthy food. We'll have a drug rehab program that actually helps people instead of padding the pockets of the owners. We'll have a small medical clinic that will focus more on the patient and less on throwing a prescription at them. We'll have therapists, support groups, education programs and even a clothing thrift shop where residents can purchase clothing with work vouchers."

"Has someone been reading too many Utopian novels? Seriously though Opal, how are you going to pay for all of this?"

"Grants, fundraising, and while the market is still hot, organic ginger. As for the novels, even the non-fiction societies failed because philosophers make terrible farmers. This is different, this isn't a society for people to join, this is a place for the lost to find a reason to really live. Just like the old Poor Farms, they can stay or leave anytime, but hopefully most will leave and leave whole. By the way, there are actually many intentional communities, the kind people join as a lifestyle choice, which are doing quite well. One of the most successful is right here in Missouri, I buy their nut butter at the grocery store down the street."

"What about your art?"

"I'll keep the studio, but I'm putting an office in the old break room of the plant. I'm leaving the desks, the chairs, even the lockers. Where the walls are gone, we'll put in glass."

"As a friend, please tell me you're not doing all of this by yourself."

"I have about a dozen volunteers and I'm applying for AmeriCorps help."

Anna dropped her pen into her purse. "Gotta go. I wish you luck and I honestly believe you can pull this off."

"Same here. I'm meeting with someone from the Downtown Merchant's Group in fifteen. They offered to make us their charity recipient for this year's Oktoberfest. I'm hoping it will be enough to make a meditation garden."

Anna slipped her purse over her shoulder and hurried through the shop and out the door. Opal rested into the thick large faux leather chair taking in five slow breathes. She silently counted, *in one, out one, in two, out two,* a thought came to her mind that she had forgotten to do a breath reset before leaving her loft, *in*

*three, out three, in four, out four, in five and out five.*
There it was, that peaceful place that brings clarity and
presence. Calm and prepared to move on to the next
item of the day, she picked up the envelope and pulled
out its contents. Garden of Grace 501c3. She flipped to
the back to the drawings as the room darkened from
passing clouds sure to bring rain. The drawings, her
drawings, her vision. She laughed quietly. It wasn't hers at
all, only her own addition to hundreds of years of ideas
filled with compassion.

---

Opal slowly walked back to her car allowing
herself to become slightly drenched from the large drops
of rain falling straight down from the sky. As she turned
the corner, she noticed a woman sitting between the bays
of the recently closed bakery. Hunkered, gaunt, her eyes
sunk into absence. "Ma'am, are you okay?" The woman
hardly moved. Opal joined her in the dank cigarette butt
covered corner, "Ma'am, are you okay?" she repeated.

"I can't find Alex."

"What's your name?"

"Mary."

"Mary, do you have somewhere safe to go?"

"Eden House, but I have to find Alex."

"Maybe Alex will find you there Mary. I can take you, but we will have to go now."

Reluctantly Mary got up and followed her to the car.

Reluctantly, Opal dropped her off and waited for her to enter the front door of the local church-ran shelter and soup kitchen. Pulling a pencil from her console she quickly wrote the words *Mary's Path* above the trail to the Meditation Garden.

Reluctantly she left as the rain ceased to fall.

# 7

# July

*My name is Gretel, I Love..... Breadcrumbs.*

"Okay, so we have a veggie-jack panini and a half berry power salad with raspberry balsamic dressing and an iced pomegranate green tea. Would you like a fruit cup or chips with that?"

The anxious young man in khaki skinny pants and dark high-tops shifted his backpack from his right shoulder to his left. He frustratingly pulled his eyes from his phone, "Um, fruit I guess."

"That will be eleven sixty-five," announced the seventeen-year-old girl with dark blonde pigtails behind the counter.

He reached into his back pocket and quickly produced a twenty-dollar bill. He hadn't looked at her once since his turn came to order.

"Eight thirty-five is your change, here's your buzzer."

His hand blindly opened to accept the change and buzzer. His fingers clutching them in auto response. He started to turn away, "Your cup sir." He shoved the change into his front pocket, the buzzer owned his right hand. He had no choice. He had to stuff his phone in the backpack in order to take the cup. It was enough of a distraction to notice. "Breadcrumbs! Okay, that's funny. Gretel, breadcrumbs. You're a funny girl."

"Hey, Goldilocks, you're out in fifteen."

Gretel rolled her eyes and called back toward the kitchen, "It's Gretel. Gretel, not Goldilocks."

"Yeah, whatever." Was all she heard. She wanted to hate him, everyone else did. But she couldn't, she wasn't able to hate anyone. Besides, she knew it was his job to be a jerk, or at least he thought being a jerk was the only way he could do his job. Either way she was glad to be let go a little early, she now had two extra hours before her parents expected her home. The new kid stood behind her holding his cash drawer, "Hi, I'm Evan, you were in my chemistry class last year, right?" Gretel pulled her own drawer and moved to the side taking a closer look, "Um, yeah. Fun class huh?"

"Not sure about fun, but I passed." Evan took command of the register while pointing at his tag,

*My name is Evan, I Love..... Coding*

Gretel forced a slight smile; she hated small talk. "Well, good luck Evan." That was the best she could do; besides, she was anxious to get clocked out.

She dropped her cash drawer off on her managers desk and continued straight on to the break room. A couple evening shift employees sat at the small square plastic table in front of the lockers silently staring at their phones. One of them murmured, "Happy Birthday, Gretel."

She uttered an even quieter "Thank you" as she tried to figure out how anyone knew. She rolled her eyes when she discovered the postcard sized paper taped to her locker.

Happy Birthday!

We think you're pretty neat

Use this card for a special

Birthday Treat!

Gretel ran through the parking lot across the hot concrete to her mid 90's faded red Dodge Neon. She turned the engine on, rolled the windows down, tossed her bag and a blueberry birthday muffin into the back seat and prepared for her fifteen-minute drive without air conditioning. The engine sputtered as she turned the key, "Come on Poppy Girl, you can do it," the engine turned with her third try, "Way to go Poppy, you just gotta make

it one more year. You get me to Saint Louis and I'll make you a permanent work of art."

---

Sue pulled the top rack of the dishwasher out as far as it would go, coffee cups on the left from back to front, drinking glasses on the right, back to front, plastic storage containers in the center. "Craig, she did say she would be home by seven, right?"

Craig yelled from the living room as he made his way to the kitchen, "Hold on, I can't hear you. Now what was that?"

"Wasn't Gretel supposed to be home by seven? We have to leave no later than seven-thirty or we'll be late. I know my parents will be early, they always are and if we're late again my dad will make some kind of crack about us having no sense of time."

Craig sat at the kitchen bar and shuffled through the stack of mail at the end, "Look at the app. Maybe she had to run an errand on her way home."

Sue wiped her hands on the towel hanging on the stove before reaching into her back pocket for her phone. "Great, she's in some kind of alley or something. What would she be doing in an alley?"

"Meth, cocaine, heroin, no- bootlegged movies. Yeah, she's selling bootlegged movies."

"Oh my God Craig, that isn't funny."

"Here, give me the phone."

Sue held it in front of him, "See?"

Using his finger Craig slid the real time map to the south, "Look, this happens all the time. There's the coffee shop, she probably got off work early and went to the coffee shop to draw for a while."

"On her birthday, when we have reservations for dinner with the whole family?"

"It's *her* birthday Sue. Just call her."

Gretel really had no choice in the matter when it came to *how* she wanted to celebrate her birthday, but she was able to choose *where*. She loved walking through the old house filled with art, statues, and colorful plants. She couldn't understand why anyone would want to eat inside but she would peak into the giant rooms filled with little round tables covered with heavy white cloth. It was what awaited her out the back door that made this place

120

one of her favorite restaurants in town. Bronze angels, cement gargoyles, fountains, and flowers, all sitting on cobblestone floors and surrounded by enough plants to create the illusion of being in the rain forest.

The long table in the center of the garden was clearly their destination. Two giant mylar balloons covered in bright pink musical notes and the words *HAPPY BIRTHDAY* bounced back and forth in the open air. Gretel whispered to her mother as they walked to the table, "Must be the doings of Aunt Lori."

"She did the decorating" Sue whispered back, "But I picked them out."

Soon the table was filled with Gretel's parents, grandparents, aunts, uncles, and cousins. Bread and oil, glasses of lemonade and wine, salads, and conversations. As the sun slowly slipped away, the dining garden became illuminated by clear tiny lights that hung from every corner. Gretel thought aloud, "Fairy lights, yeah.... fairy lights." Her young cousin giggled and whispered back at the thought, "Fairy lights?"

"Oh, um, it's a project I'm working on. Just collecting ideas."

"What kind of project Gretel?" Her grandfather seemed to only hear when she wished he wouldn't.

Sue heard the question from the other end of the table, "Gretel is in charge of putting together two of the half-time shows this year Dad. Tell everyone about that honey, it's so ingenious."

Gretel sighed with relief, "Um, so we're doing a space themed half-time show with a few songs from space movies like Star Wars. One of them we're going to end as a constellation and the other a spaceship. It's pretty cool Grandpa."

"They do it different now than when I was in high school," Craig pushed his empty salad plate to the side, giddy to talk about band in the old days. "Back then we marched, knees up and in straight lines, pivot turns, almost a military style march. Today, they sort of dance."

"And *we* have to memorize our music and steps, you guys used lyres."

"Speaking of marching band, I have a surprise announcement." Sue pulled her giant purse from the back of her chair and dug inside to find a stack of colorful pamphlets she had saved for just the right moment. "We're going on a trip this weekend!" She handed the pamphlets to the right, "Pass this around Mom. These are the TOP four music art schools in the state. We have two appointments Saturday and two Sunday. I bet they'll be fighting over her."

Amid the *oohs and ahhs*, Gretel stared at her mother in dismay. "Mom, I have to work this weekend. Band camp starts Monday morning so I can't work my regular shift anymore. The only hours I can get are on the weekends."

"Your job cannot force you to work instead of pursuing a college education Gretel."

"They'll fire me or make me quit."

"So be it. I don't know why you insist on working there anyways. You need to be devoting every extra minute you have to practicing and keeping up your GPA, that's the only way you get scholarships."

She felt like she couldn't breathe. She felt suffocated and angry. The words simply wouldn't come to her to respond.

"We have a grilled salmon with summer veggies," the tall thin waitress in thick black slacks and a white starched shirt held the steaming plate toward the table.

Gretel raised her hand, "That's me."

Alone in her room, Gretel pulled her birthday gifts out of their shiny glittery bags and piled them at the end of her bed. A music themed journal, phone case and socks and a large white plastic treble clef with a G in the center. She knew something was missing... Aunt Lori's gift. Under the stack of pink and ivory tissue paper, she found the little box. *Leave it to Aunt Lori,* she thought as she carefully hung the silver necklace around her neck and held the tiny silver toad that dangled from the end. She smiled as she recalled how horrified her cousins were by her fondness of catching toads and insisting they were her pets. It was always Aunt Lori that found some way to celebrate everyone in a way that no one else could.

The starship formation made of a hundred x's on a graph glowed from her laptop on her bedroom desk. She did enjoy the process; she loved band and carried the role of drum major as an honor. She pulled the computer to her lap humming the powerful spacey sounding song as she imagined the x's moving around the graph. She closed her eyes and opened them, maybe her mom was right, maybe it was best to go after what you're already good at.

She opened a new tab and typed; *What to do in Forest Park.* Unfortunately, Forest Park wasn't on the itinerary for the weekend.

Four p.m. was the perfect time to be at the coffee shop for a teenage introvert. The late afternoon crowd was smaller than during breakfast and lunch hours and primarily filled with other more extroverted teenagers. She enjoyed the energy of people around her and at the same time, enjoyed having no obligation to speak to them. Gretel had a few fairly close friends at school, but none she confided in. To her the only things her contemporaries shared about their personal lives were the things of unnecessary drama. Gretel preferred to stick with simple facts when asked, *how are you?* Her responses typically went something like this, *Good, on my way to English Lit* or *Good, are you going to the movies with everyone tonight?* When faced with anyone sharing something personal with her she usually responded with an appropriate *That sucks* or *That's great.* The one thing she was good at, however, was allowing for advice when she really needed it, though she rarely asked. When a kind, soft voice behind her spoke, "You look perplexed my dear." Gretel was more than willing to respond.

"I actually am, Eliza." She pulled her giant bag off the chair in front of her as a gesture to invite her *partner in crime* to visit. "I have a conundrum."

"Alright, let's have it." Eliza plopped her notebook and pen down in front of her putting its use on hold.

125

"My parents scheduled college visits for this weekend to four music arts schools. I told them I had to work and couldn't go, so my mom called my boss and talked him into giving me the weekend off."

"You obviously haven't told them."

"Nope."

"Getting a music major would be a wonderful thing to do with your life Gretel, if that's what you want. But if it isn't, you're going to have to tell them and the sooner the better."

Gretel stared at the words on her journal, *fairy lights.* "Okay, I will, um, I need to run to the Garden Shop. Can you meet me at the project? I need to get it finished by tomorrow night."

Eliza laughed, "Now that I can do. I'm not the best candidate for mother-daughter relationship advice. No, I'm not much for any relationship advice." Eliza picked her notebook and coffee back up to make her way to her regular seat in the front window. "I'll meet you there in half an hour, I have a chapter or two sitting in my head just waiting to get on this parchment. The gnomes are planning a trip to the homeland," She leaned into Gretel's ear and whispered, "You know they've been gone for over three-hundred years."

The hot July sun poured across the pavement creating a mirage of water waving across the wide dark road. Gretel wiped the sweat from her cheeks leaving a streak of mud across her face. Eliza sang to herself where the neighboring brick building blocked the setting sun, "Sitting in the garden, playing in the shade, hiding in the marigolds, until the sun does fade."

"Did you just make that up Eliza?" Gretel asked as she held a watering can over a patch of daisies intentionally dumping some on her feet.

"The fairies taught me that one! Their wings lose their luster in direct sunlight, but you know that."

Gretel laughed. She didn't know that, but then again, she had only read the first two of Eliza's new series of books. "Eliza! Do you hear that? The band started the second half of the show. They'll be done in half an hour."

Eliza jumped up and made her best attempt at a jitterbug, "In the mood, that's what they tell me.... You go on ahead, I can finish it from here."

Gretel wiped her hand off on her t-shirt. There wasn't time to make herself presentable. She thanked Eliza, threw her large cotton patchwork bag onto her shoulders, and started walking toward the farmers market, toward the music. It was only three blocks, but three blocks with a 102* heat index is a long walk. She was glad to have her reusable bottle almost full of water and found it empty by the time she reached the market.

Sue was in the front row, foot tapping and shoulders swaying. Gretel jokingly referred to the entire row as the *spouse spot,* all the husbands and wives of the band members sat there for every concert like swing band groupies. Gretel walked far to the side and waved at her mother who waved back, surprised to see her there. Sue held up two fingers to let her know there were only two songs left in the set. She carefully managed her way through the local swing club dancers to the back of the market to refill her water bottle. It was comfortable in the market; all the side walls were opened allowing a breeze to pour through the long multi-purpose rectangle. *This is art*, she thought, *its own kind of art that sings its own song.*

*One O'clock Jump* barely ended before her dad's band's signature end song *Moonlight Serenade* began. The clapping drowned out the first few notes of the song while the dancers happily rested their heads on their partners shoulders and gently carried each other slowly across the dusty concrete floor. The final notes faded in a decrescendo with each instrument holding one note, all eyes on the director awaiting her to signal an end to the fermata, an end to another evening of bringing audible joy for no reason other than because everyone there.....loved music. The clapping resumed the moment the conductor's arms left the air and her hands joined together at her stomach. She turned around to the audience and bowed, she turned back to the band raising her hands upward signaling them to all stand and bow as well, she turned back to the audience sweeping her hands and she walked to the edge of the stage. The clapping didn't stop, the audience stood as the clapping intensified until the band sat back down and only the sound of quiet chatter and folding chairs being drug across the concrete remained. Gretel was sure the mud on her face was streaked with her tears. She wiped her face with the bottom of her t-shirt and ran toward her father who stood at the front of the short plank stage.

"Gretel! I didn't know you were here; I was just telling Joe here about the formations you're working on."

"Hi Joe." She grabbed her father's oboe case and held it toward him, "Dad I have to show you and mom something, but we have to go now."

Craig and Sue spent the first block talking about the concert and how great an idea it was to invite the dance club. Gretel nodded her head and threw in an occasional *uh huh* and *totally agree.* As they turned the corner to the final two-block stretch she had no choice but to intervene. "I have to tell you something, about what I'm going to show you..... it's important." She checked her phone, eight-thirty-two, the perfect amount of time. "Come on, there's a park bench over here."

Sue and Craig looked at each other in fear, she could only imagine what they were thinking. She laughed silently to herself imagining her mother thinking something ridiculous like her being pregnant or announcing she was running away with the circus. "It's all good, I promise. Here, sit."

They both reluctantly sat on the bench looking slightly less terrified but with enough concern Gretel wasted no time. She stood in front of them with the speech she had been writing in her mind for months.

"See these buildings? They're like music, they're art. They tell a story; they represent a specific time in history and culture. Just like tonight's concert brought our community together, so do our downtowns with little shops that sell things you can't get at superstores, and restaurants and coffee shops where you know the names of the people who bring you your food and coffee. When we can walk on our feet to all the places we love, surrounded by all of this brick and mortar, this character..." She realized her voice was rising, she realized how good it felt.

"Gretel, I've never seen you so passionate about something. Can you tell us what this is all about?" Craig's eyes were as big as his smile was wide.

"I'm sorry. I just, I didn't know how to tell you. I...I don't want a degree in music, don't get me wrong I love music, but I love this, and I believe in it. I want to make places like this even better." She guzzled the remaining water from the bottle and took a deep breathe. "I applied to a university for a degree in Landscape Architecture and I had to submit a finished project as a part of the application. I finished it tonight so I could show you."

Sue gripped Craig's hand, "We just didn't want you to look back on your life in thirty years and wish you had pursued a career in music."

"Dad, you didn't need a *degree in* music to bring joy to people's life *with* music. You do that like once a week! Besides, you love your job at the Post Office, and if you never worked there you wouldn't have met mom and there wouldn't be a me."

Craig shook his head in agreement, in a means of respect his daughter always knew was there though she never knew how to ask for its proof. "Let's go see this project."

---

Craig, Sue, and Gretel stood on the sidewalk looking toward a wide empty spot between two two-story brick Italianate shops. "It's called an infill lot, so there used to be two buildings here, a bank and a dress shop. The bank fell down, and no one took the time to realize that it was holding up the dress shop, that's how they used to build them. A few years ago, the dress shop fell down too. Gretel took them each by the hand, "Okay, close your eyes!" She slowly walked them to the other side of the building, "You can open them now!"

Sue couldn't help but awe at the scene before her, "It's beautiful Gretel! Beautiful!" Just as they began to enter the micro-garden, solar powered fairy lights lit the paths below them. Suddenly, blue sparkling lights shot out from the center of the garden as the sound of Chopin's *Spring Waltz* flowed from every corner. Tiny fairies with glowing wings attached to statues of giant frogs, tiny deer and colorful mushrooms appeared that *danced* to the beat of the music. Shepherd hooks held luminous acorns, white iron benches sat nestled between thick patches of coneflowers, daisies, hollyhocks, and poppy mallows. Happy little gnomes holding fiddles and

flutes hid beneath birdbaths with color changing fountains. Craig smiled with pride when he found the small sign set on a plain white music stand giving *his* daughter credit for the amazing place that almost lost purpose.

**Fairy Tale Symphony**
**Micro Garden**

**Designed by**
**Gretel Louise Bachmann**

**Sponsored by**
**Annabelle's Garden Shop**
**Uptown Music**
**The Tagalongs Book**
**Series by Eliza Manning**

The three sat on one of the little iron benches until the music stopped and the lights went out. Hand in hand, Craig and Sue slowly left the garden with the feeling they had just emerged from the pages of a Hans Christian

Anderson book. With nothing left but the sound of crickets and distant cars they walked along the sidewalk by the light of a few streetlights and a crescent moon. Silently, contently, dreaming of all the empty spaces that *Gretel* could turn into places.

# 8

# August

The dark cloud pours

In from the west

Quickly

Spinning

Growing


Day becomes night

The clock tower casts its shadow

On all below


The shops

The restaurants

The diners

The brick and plaster


Business as usual

Goes on without notice

While the dark cloud sags into the panes

Pours into the happy and the mindless

A twinge of discomfort

A sense of the eerie

A shudder of the nerves


The ink spills onto the paper

Over and over

For the few purists of word


The coffee shop songs

Beautifully deep

Become as dark as the cloud

That slowly creeps


The suits check the ink

And remark of the weather

The unusual chill

That has suddenly entered

The latte flower

Blown by the breeze

Resembles something

So near a beast


The cloud begins churning

Spitting lightning

As it roars

While the suits stir

In their seats

Keeping their eyes to the doors


As quickly as it came

So quickly it left


And everyone looked

To the ink of the press


The sunflowers so regal

Though their glory put aside

For there's much to speak of

By those who type

Whilst they hide


Oh, haven't you heard?

Oh, didn't you know?

I was told firsthand by

So and So


The elections are coming

The stump is live streaming

Suddenly, suddenly

Everyone is scheming


Chaos abounds

The cloud lifts as it giggles

While seats of new suits

Twist as they sizzle

9

# September

Quinn stared at the blank document on the screen. He swiveled his chair to look out the window of his office into the empty narrow street facing the backside of elderly structures and half-empty parking lots. He checked his email. He wasn't expecting anything important; it was just one more distraction from having to work. Nothing new in the inbox, only a calendar reminder- *Pulse of the Heartland deadline-6 p.m.* It was too quiet. He flipped the top of the laptop down and tucked it into the center of his backpack. He yanked the cord from the outlet behind him, grabbed his notebook and three pens from his center drawer then shoved them in next to the laptop. He looked at his watch, 9:30 a.m.

The coffee shop was buzzing with people standing in line, people at the window counters, and the back corner tables. A blend of folk music and conversation, Quinn stood in line behind a woman in running attire with a jogging stroller. He peeked into the stroller to see the bright-eyed, content pudgy baby. The child's mother smiled at him as she pushed the stroller forward two feet and focused her eyes on the menu. He had seen her there many times before. He thought about seeing her coming in with what he assumed to be work friends a few years before. A year later he noticed her rounding belly growing by the day. He thought about how everyone who entered often enough might feel like the omniscient observer the same way he did. He imagined being there in another five years and seeing her and a little boy, a little boy he could nearly claim he had known before he was born.

"Next. Quinn, I can take your order."

He quickly moved to the counter, realizing had he been driving the guy behind him might have honked and accused him of being on his phone at a red light. "Morning Elena! Sorry about that, got lost in my thoughts."

She laughed, "No problem, Quinn, your usual?"

"Yeah, let's start with fully leaded, I'll need a tab today."

"Deadline day huh?"

"6:30."

"I'll have it out in just a minute, good luck!"

Quinn's usual table was occupied, so he took the next table down. It wasn't that he preferred the location as much as they were the only two tables near outlets to plug in his computer besides the high-tops. He opened the laptop, situated it as best as he could for comfortable typing, set his coffee to the right, his notebook, and pens to the left and tucked the nearly empty backpack into an empty chair. Once again, he stared at the blank screen. His mind began to sing along to the song playing through the shop. The thirty something man next to him joyfully greeted his guest, "Do anything fun this weekend?" The younger woman announced her reply as she took the seat on the other side of the table, "A bunch of us did a wine tour, made a whole day of it." Quinn thought about his weekend, taking the kids out east to pick apples. He thought about his drive to the office, his walk to the coffee shop, finally it began.

*So hot and humid, without the subtle signs only nature can provide, no one would recognize that summer had entered her final phase of the year.*

*From the one stop light on 24 Highway in Buckner east far beyond the county line, September's glory causes one's breath to halt. Missouri's springtime neon green has now been replaced by fading leaves on all the trees to a comforting Golden Hue. Pale in its majesty as it slowly turns to summer's end and embraces autumn's glory. The highway provides an awestruck view of rolling hills and scattered villages. Corn and soy paled and dried, soon for the taking... Golden gleams of a place in time.*

*The goldfinches have left the patches of brown*
*sagging sunflower heads and relentless Johnson*
*Grass. What is left of the garden has gone to seed*
*except for the endless sprawls of pumpkin vines*
*as the giant fruits that hide beneath the leaves*
*begin to turn to orange. The sun departs from the*
*day by seven-thirty and wakes the next nearly the*
*same.*

His cup was empty. He took a caffeine assessment and determined he could have one more before switching to decaf and adding a water. A large group of older men had gathered at the large center table. He listened to their conversations bounce back and forth from politics to the economy and finally the weather, how bad a year it was for corn, how the Chinese aren't buying the soy anyways. It reminded him of the roadside dive he and the kids stopped at for breakfast before apple picking. He recalled the trucks in the parking lot, he thought about the long table filled with men in overalls and Veteran baseball caps, camouflage jackets and NFL t-shirts.

*The farmers meet by six for coffee and*
*biscuits and gravy in little restaurants in every little*
*town. They talk about the rain, they talk about*

145

*who lost nearly everything in the flood of March
and who lost the rest in the flood of May. They
talk about who risked it all and planted again.
They talk about how everyone is praying that a
freeze holds off for at least another month,
because so much of the soybeans haven't had
time to dry and so much of the corn has yet to
fall.*

Quinn's table had emptied. He nonchalantly
moved his belongings over and slipped into the bench.
He knew it was a bit ridiculous to have a sense of
ownership over a public table, and still silently celebrated
as a middle-aged man in a suit slapped down a brightly
colored chart at the table he had so quickly vacated.

*In little coffee shops in little downtowns,
the businessmen and women gather with their
laptops and binders over pumpkin spice and
caramel lattes to lay out their goals for the coming
year. They know they're speculating. Amid the
smallest achievement they remind each other of
all the factors the economists have been
repeating since economists existed. Low interest
rates, skilled labor shortages, trends and the oh so*

*dreaded election year. And yet, there is a foreign sense of calm and peace in the air.*

*In every breakroom, from the manufacturers to the librarians, the conversations find themselves immersed in the same topics. Football, play by play. Every injury, every pass, and every tackle. Everyone is a referee, everyone is a coach, and everyone is sure they know exactly how the season will play out. Everyone is talking about what festivals the weekends will bring, apple festivals, pecan festivals, Oktoberfests just weeks away. Some have put up their summer clothes for the year and brought out the bins of winter clothes. Many of the men talk about hunting season, when they're going, where they're going (but only in generality, hunting deer is much the same as hunting for mushrooms, exact locations are never revealed). The women especially talk about their favorite hearty meals, specifically the kinds that are cooked in a slow cooker. The grilling season is coming to its end, the season of stews and soups is soon to commence.*

"Quinn! How are you, my friend?" Quinn looked up to see a dark-haired woman in blue jeans and a heavy seaweed green sweater standing in front of him. He knew this could happen, he expected it. He was only one of dozens of regulars that either knew each other because of the coffee shop or sometimes even knew each other before they had discovered the little community living room. "Mira, how the heck are you? How's Fifty Mile Distributing doing?"

Mira sat down on half of the seat in front of her signaling she didn't plan to stay very long. "Great Quinn, really great. Thank you again for the awesome review last month, we got four more customers out of that."

"Really? That's, that's fantastic Mira. What brings you to the coffee shop today?"

"I'm meeting Isabell to go over the Oktoberfest. We're donating pumpkins for the carving contest." She pulled a thick glossy card from her purse, "See, official sponsors."

"Wow, that's just around the corner huh? They're giving the proceeds to that new homeless project, at the um, the old Parker Electronics factory, right?"

"Yeah, I couldn't think of a better cause." Mira looked toward the front door of the shop, "Hey, Liz is here, good to see you, Quinn!"

"Good to see you, Mira! Say hi to Austin for me, okay?"

"You bet." And off she went to meet Liz and her two boys standing in line. He placed his hands back on the computer keys, barely tapping the F and J. It was no use. He needed a break anyways, his legs felt stiff, and his back had grown a slight ache. He looked at the time at the bottom right corner of the screen, 12:25, *yeah*, he thought, *it was lunchtime*. He packed everything up and headed for the door, "Done already?" Elena called from the counter. "Not quite yet" he laughed, "I'll be back."

Quinn walked down the street in search of lunch. He stopped in front of the empty bakery with the giant For Lease sign. He shook his head and kept going. He crossed over to the new restaurant in town, Doyle's Irish Pub. He figured he could kill two birds with one stone, eat and have a revue to submit to the metro food magazine. The lunch crowd was filtering out as Quinn made his way in. He liked the look of it, cozy and inviting. Small square tables with thick green tablecloths filled the long narrow room. He took a seat at the old-world bar and began memorizing the scene. A Killian's Irish Red mirror hung in the center of the glass shelved back bar. The entire restaurant was filled with Irish themed paintings, wooden plaques with Irish sayings and framed posters of Irish brand whiskeys, liqueurs, gins, and beer. A stocky man wearing a white button-up shirt with the sleeves rolled to his elbows set a napkin and glass of ice-water down in front of him, "Menu's on the board, clam chowder's on special today. What can I get you to drink?" Quinn had heard it was a family from New England that started the place, the bar tender's accent confirmed the coffee shop rumor. "I'm good with the water, thanks." "Alright, I'll be back in a minute for your order." The chowder sounded good, Irish stew sounded even better, but he couldn't get Mira's mention of the old factory off his mind. He never really paid any attention to it, just drove by in his usual workday hurry every so often on the way to somewhere else. He realized he never really paid any attention to the homeless people it would eventually house, they were just there, like trees and empty Styrofoam cups along the sidewalks, part of the landscape. "I'll have an Irish grilled cheese to go."

---

Quinn sat in his car watching the steady stream of carpenters, plumbers, and electricians shuffle in and out of the old factory to their work vans and back. He watched a small crew of prisoners erecting a gazebo over a large circle of mulch off to the side of the building. He ate the last bite of the sandwich as the words began to

form, the words that might push the envelope just a little bit, even for *Pulse of the Heartland.*

The coffee shop was nearly emptied in its mid-afternoon lull. Quinn got his table back. Elena knew it was time for decaf.

> *This is life in the Midwest. This is business as usual for those of us that have known nothing else. At the end of the day, we all drive home. Beyond the tall nineteenth century brick gems that comprise our old downtowns, the Victorian era monuments that we tend to assume represented the era for all. Beyond the tiny square bungalows with their perfectly centered dormers and the little post war neighborhoods filled with simple tract ranches and split levels. Beyond the fading two - story homes of the 90's covered in brown and tan vinyl siding, and the newest gilded expression, the non-symmetric McMansions strategically placed just minutes from Walmart, Starbucks and CVS. Beyond the people we don't want to see. The people that make us nervous, the people who aimlessly walk about us as if aliens. The people with heavy bags and backpacks. The people pushing shopping*

*carts alongside the highway. The people who look lost and unfed. Sometimes we wonder, where did they come from, how did they get to this state, and where will they go when winter comes?*

He tipped his coffee cup to his mouth without looking at it. Empty. He knew he was almost done and made his final trip for the day to the counter for his last refill and to pay the tab. He felt a woosh of cool air as a woman came in carrying a heavy box full of honey using her hip to push through the door. "Almost feels like fall this afternoon. Want these in the back?" Elena answered while she filled Quinn's cup, "Yeah Holly, how many did you bring?"

"Six."

"I'll be back in a second and get you a check."

Quinn dug his cell phone out of the backpack and texted the babysitter, *I'm taking the rest of the day off. I'll be home in time for the bus."*

*During this yearly equinox, as the calm winds slowly seep in from the north, as we drive along these rolling meadows of gold, sometimes we suddenly find ourselves falling off the daily treadmill. We ignore the calls, we turn off the news, we sit on the porch with that precious seasonal flannel and simply watch the sun go down.*

*Deep in the few wooded places left near the highways and the towns, the lost and unfed settle into their makeshift tents with their plastic bags filled with day old carbs from the non-profits. I don't know what they're thinking, but I am sure that in this moment, in the Golden splendor of September, they too have found awe in the same sunset.*

~ Quinn Bristow

# 10

# October

October in Missouri can mask itself as nearly any season before the month's end. It often begins by teasing the Autumn enthusiast with cool darkened days and tumultuous rains. Just as everyone has put up their open-toed shoes and pulled out leather boots and thick flannel jackets, she turns and giggles as summer returns. One morning might dip into the upper 30's while a few days later only get down to the mid 70's before the dawn. Whatever the weather, the tell-tale signs of Autumn cannot be disguised. The sun rises later, often in the mystery of fog and sets sooner on slowly turning forests of gold and reddening leaves. There is something about the angle of the sun in October that will send the evening sky to pick the most beautiful place to set aglow. Particularly atop fields of fading goldenrod interspersed with Frost Asters that only upon close inspection could be deemed a weed.

October 4th was one of those in-between days. *Thursday, October 4th, 5:57 am. 61\*. Calm, not too humid. Sold 18 bottles of honey, 5 dozen eggs, 3 jars of jam and about half the produce yesterday at the farmer's market. Abigail is flying in tomorrow for the weekend. Cleaned her room up last week. It is still full of things, and yet so empty. Nick's room is still Nick's room. Even though the walls are now golden yellow his glow in the dark stars still cover the ceiling.*

*Will is bringing a half cord of wood home after work tonight. Looks like we'll need a fire by Sunday. Probably have the A/C back on in a week. I feel good this morning, energetic....but off just a little. Like something is off.*

Holly set her pen down on a small wooden table next to her journal as the sound of the giant yellow diesel crept down the curve. The bus stopped at the same spot it had for who knows how many years. Just as the sun was cresting the eastern horizon it pulled into the neighbor's drive with its bright red stop sign flipped out to the side. The door opened, soon after three eager children disappeared as the door closed and the sign fell back to the yellow. She could imagine her old motherly lab standing at the curb to watch the bus take the children away from her for the day. Imagine the loving dog meander back to the same spot every afternoon at 4:15 like clockwork. Miss Sophie, always one step ahead of their arrival back home.

Her coffee was getting cold. The air was getting cold. At least the birds were singing. The chickens cackled that horrible sound of impending eggs while the roosters competed in their calls of morning reign. The cat let out a sweet meow of notification that she had chosen to visit as she reached both front paws onto Holly's robe.

157

"Good morning, Daisy. I see you have been adventuring." Daisy's furry white feet were covered in black ash, a sure sign she had been out hunting in the burn pile. Holly got the hint, "I'll be right back pretty girl." She grabbed the cool cup of coffee and Daisy's food bowl. Cup in the microwave, bowl dipped deep into the bag of cat food. As she sat on the couch waiting for the coffee to be rewarmed, she stared at the blank television on the wall. Turning it off during the day, getting rid of the satellite, that was her idea ten years ago. Now it was just streamed documentaries and borrowed library movies. But again, that was when Miss Sophie brought the kids home at 4:15. For just a second, she reconsidered the decision. She missed those old sounds. Even if they included arguments about who was responsible for the upstairs bathroom being a mess or who's turn it was to take out the compost. They were sounds none-the-less.

Daisy immediately took to emptying her bowl of fish-shaped mystery bits while Holly attempted to resume her journaling. To her absolute joy, the phone rang.

"Hey Buddy!"

"Mamma, I got coffee ready! You workin' the market today?"

"No market today, just gotta drop off half a dozen bottles of honey at the coffee shop at some point and

Fifty Mile Distribution is picking up an order at three.
Give me twenty to check the goats and I'll be right there!"

For Holly, morning coffee on Nick's back porch
was the best way to start the day. Her house sat high on
the flat, beautiful in its own way it sprawled with field for
500 feet before the forest began and descended to the
creek. The only trees near the house were those she and
Will planted. There would have been more had the
county not required a nearly half acre septic system.
Nick's house sat just below the ridge on the other side of
her, as the crow flies. On the deck they could stare at
what seemed to be a never-ending rise of forest. On the
front porch the Little Blue River, only a few hundred feet
away. Better yet, it was time with Nick. Being only a few
minutes' drive, she would be there every day, but you
simply don't do that to newlyweds. So, she arrived by
choice on invitation only.

Hiking boots, pajama purposed sweatpants and a
thick lined flannel was sufficient to travel one half mile to
the society free safety of visiting one's son. North straight
downhill with a sharp west curve, one turn on the edge of
the river and she landed the old brown Ford truck behind
the simple though adoring 1906 Craftsman bungalow.
Nick stood on the deck wearing his best overalls, a pair of
worn-down cowboy boots and his own thick flannel shirt.
His morning hair made Holly laugh. "Good morning

son, I see you still have your Araucana chicken hair this morning!"

"Yep. And I still blame your DNA for that."

"Since I haven't seen your father's hair in 30 years, I suppose I'll take the blame."

"Let's get you some coffee."

"Please."

Holly followed Nick through the mudroom and into the kitchen. She looked around to see if anything had changed since being there last. "I see you and Alyssa got the cube thing put up."

"Yep, I'm turnin' out to be a pretty good honey-do kind of husband Mama. And it's an organizer, not a cube thing. Alyssa corrected me on that last night."

Holly laughed as she carefully picked through the coffee cups in the cupboard looking for the one that most resembled how she felt. It was an odd behavior that she couldn't explain and told no one about. She chose her clothes that way, she chose her food that way and didn't question it. Her philosophy was simple, embrace yourself for who you are, even the odd parts.

The deck didn't disappoint. They sat silent for a moment as steam poured from their coffee cups and their breath vaporized into the cool morning air. A crow screamed as she flew from the top of the ridge toward the river, her sound echoing through the trees. Nick whispered, "Mom, look" as he pointed toward the south. A beautiful doe still in her red summer coat and her spotless fawn had carefully crept out of the woods into the pasture, oblivious to any human being nearby. They were cautious, as the mother kept her white tail in a continuous twitch but comfortable enough to enjoy a morning snack of dew-covered clover. The moment lasted just long enough for Nick to get a couple of pictures of the duo on his phone.

"It's fatten up time for them."

"It's fatten up time for all of us." Holly added as she flattened her glove covered hands over her stomach. "Seriously though, my appetite doubles in the fall, every year, always has."

"Mama, you know what happens to me in the fall. The same thing that happens to dad. We're both incapable of thinking about anything but being in a tree stand with our bows. It's the primal hunter and gatherer in all of us."

"I'm afraid that you and dad belong to a small percentage that have any actual connection to your, well, primal inner self. We're all too busy being distracted by things that don't matter to have a clue what we're experiencing on our primal levels."

Nick laughed, "Yep, dad and I aren't hunting for profile pictures, we're hunting for...."

It was a sound. A somewhat loud sound, something like a girl maybe. A scream maybe. A scream from a girl who was playing maybe.

Neither said anything. Nick took both their cups back into the house to refill them with coffee. "Is it supposed to rain?"

Holly reluctantly dug her phone from her bag that she purposely hung on the top of the deck steps. She swiped up, across, then tapped to see the forecast. "Looks like there's a pretty serious cold front moving in from the north. We have a 70% chance of storms." She returned the phone back to the bag haphazardly dropping it into the center.

The sparsely colored leaves on the trees shook as the wind picked up, the sky slowly darkening as the front slowly moved east over the river. Soon the shadow grew to cover the house all the way to the ridge.

"The *tree* lost its leaves yesterday. Had them all or at least nearly all in the morning and by the time the sun went down all but a few were on the ground. I didn't realize it until I put the chickens up. Everything looked so different I had to stop and figure out why. You know a Chinese Empress tree can grow twenty feet its first year? I guess the pods used to be used like packing foam back in the day. The seeds would fly out of the boxes on the trains."

"Aw mom, come on you know you love that tree." Nick laughed.

"I suppose I would if it were anywhere else, but it blocks my beautiful view! I can't see the pond from the dining room or the kitchen window anymore. I have to run upstairs to see it." She sipped the quickly cooling coffee. "No matter now until May. Just a trunk and branches. Besides it's invasive, we're not supposed to let them grow."

"Mom, we're invasive."

"That's true."

"We kill armadillo's because they tear up our fields, the ones that we created by clear cutting a forest. We hire sharpshooters to kill deer because they cause car accidents, but we text and drive. We kill any animal that is overpopulated because *we're* overpopulated...."

163

The sound was different. Blood curdling different. Terrifyingly horrible. They looked at each other frozen, unable to move, unable to think. They said nothing, just jumped from their seats simultaneously. They ran down the driveway, toward the river and back. They stopped.

"Mom, that was a..."

She interrupted, breathlessly, "A woman. She sounded like she was being... Oh God."

Nick instructed Holly to stay on the deck as he ran inside the house. She grabbed her bag and ran to her car, locking herself inside. By the time she was able to find her phone from the bottom of her bag Nick had returned. She got out quietly, phone and keys in hand, silently locking the car from the inside. She whispered, "It sounded like it came from the other side of the river."

Nick whispered back, "What I got too. You want to stay here? I have to go look for her."

"Hell no."

He looked around, his hand in his pocket. She knew he would grab his pistol.

They walked to the road, to the bridge and to the other side. The other side, the swath of property owned by someone somewhere, but not there. The swath of property the sheriff's deputy knew all too well. The swath of property favored by those without trash service as a midnight dumping spot.

The cold wind whipped through them as they entered the woods. Holly pulled the hood of her jacket up over her head. Nick tapped her shoulder, they stopped.

"Hello?" "Hello?" "Anyone here?" He yelled, keeping his hand in his pocket. They kept walking.

They heard a rustle. As a 30's something stocky man emerged out of what seemed to be no-where, Nick gripped the inside of his coat. Before either of them could say anything, the man announced himself, "I can be here. They said I can be here." He pointed toward the north side of the river, "All my stuff see, it's up there. Got kicked out and they said I can be here."

Neither asked who *they* were. He seemed nervous, which made them both feel nervous as well.

Nick pulled Holly back by the sleeve of her coat, "Hey man, um, you hear a scream? A woman scream?"

The man paced, "No."

"You sure you didn't hear a woman scream?"

"See, my wife and daughter they're in the truck it's back that way." He pointed south.

Nick pushed Holly further back, his hand remaining in the pocket. "Look man, we heard a woman scream. I'm afraid some woman was hurt, real bad. You didn't hear anything?"

"Oh, yeah. My dog perked her ears up. Yeah, I guess I heard something. They said I can be here."

"Alright man, thanks. You stay safe, okay?"

The man started to walk away. Nick grabbed Holly for the last time, pulling her backwards out of the woods until he was out of sight. Nick whispered for the last time, "We're going to run now mom, okay?"

---

The rain was coming down heavily when the Sheriff department's two marked cars and one black

unmarked car arrived. The sweet smell of burning cedar
and oak poured over the roof of the old house sinking
nearly to the ground and tried it's best to make it back up
the ridge only to turn part way up and return back down
again.

Nick played the sound from the video his security
camera captured. After he shared the story of the odd
woodland encounter, all three cars left to the other side
of the river. One car returned about a half an hour later
with news that the man had a warrant, the wife and
daughter were there and safe. That was it.

---

While Nick spent the rest of the day combing the
ridge, Holly had to get back to her *farm chores*, milking
the goats, feeding the chickens, and making honey
deliveries all before three. Fifty Mile Distribution made
quick work of filling the back of their van with Holly's
prized pie pumpkins and four boxes of Winesap apples.
She checked her phone several times each hour as the
sound of the screams haunted her the entire day.
Nothing, Nick had found nothing.

---

Will drove the truck straight past the driveway, through the front yard and stopped at the woodpile. He tossed the three heavy logs holding down the tarp, pealed the tarp back and began unloading the back of the truck. Holly grabbed her work gloves and ran out the back door to join him.

Holly took hold of a log at the edge of the tailgate and tossed it into the pile, "Did you get Nick's text? With the video?"

"Sorry, busy day." He was in his *work zone* and had only one thing on his mind, to get the wood off his truck and piled so he could eat dinner and start his weekend.

"I had coffee at Nick's this morning, and we heard a woman scream, a blood-curdling scream. We even had the sheriff come out, well, there was this scary guy living in the woods by the river...that's a longer story."

He stopped and looked at her, "What in the hell are you talking about?"

"We heard a woman scream, it sounded like she was being murdered. He got it on his security camera."

Will pushed a few logs out of the way and sat on the tailgate to watch the video. "You said you called the sheriff?"

"Yeah, they didn't find a woman, just a guy with a warrant, there's more but..."

"We can finish this later. Go get a good flashlight and I'll meet you in your truck."

---

Nick and Alyssa were nowhere to be found in or around the house. Will made a bird call and waited. About five seconds later the same call faintly returned from the north-east corner of the ridge. Will reached out for Holly's hand, "Come on, I'll help you."

Ten minutes and two more bird calls were all it took to find Nick and Alyssa sitting on a large rock below a giant burr oak. "Did you find anything?" Holly asked though nearly out of breath from the climb.

Nick nodded his head in a dismal way. "I did." He got up from the rock and walked to the other side of the tree, "Here, in the mud. I think I found her."

Pressed deep into the hillside was a footprint as large as Holly's hand. Four large egg-shaped toes above a large split triangular palm. Will shook his head in disbelief.

"Look up Dad." Will turned the flashlight straight up toward the tree.

Hanging from the crook of the tree were what looked to be the remains of a rabbit.

"I don't understand." Holly stepped onto a large anvil shaped rock to get a closer look, "What does this have to do with the woman and how did that get up there?"

Alyssa put her arm around Holly, "It wasn't a *woman*, it was a female mountain lion, a cougar."

"I thought they didn't live here."

"As far as we know, they don't Mom. They used to though. She was probably just moving through."

"Looking for a mate." Will turned the flashlight to the paw print, "That's what the scream was, it was her."

The dark sky flashed from distant lightning as a cold rush of air cut through the trees. Will pointed the flashlight forward, "Better get back to that firewood."

A whitetail buck stepped over bags of clothing scattered about the woods to rub his antlers deep into the sides of a small cedar.

A woman and her daughter settled into their room. A safe, warm room, filled with hope.

A great horned owl perched high atop a telephone pole let out a loud hooooooot, hoot, hoot, over a grid of houses below him.

A middle-aged man, still in his uniform of blue made it to the edge of the field to see his son play the last quarter of the game.

A thick, fat groundhog dug just a little deeper beneath the foundation of a fast-food restaurant that she chose for her winter home.

The fluffy white cat curled up to the edge of the hearth as Will added another log to the fire causing the flames to dance against the glass of the woodstove. Holly stepped outside as the sound of the cougar replayed in her mind. It was silent and cold. The clouds gave way to a sliver of a waning moon.

# 11
# November

Vans, SUV's, cars, even small buses- all the engines started at exactly 6:30 a.m. Carolyn stepped outside of the front door of her wide brick ranch and was met by a crisp cold breeze of impending winter. She ran back inside, grabbed her jacket from the coat hanger. Don already had his tossed behind his shoulder. "You just never know." Once she reached her old van in the driveway and was out of shadows, she was quickly warmed by the sun as if autumn had whispered, *I'm still here.* Don blew her a kiss as he slipped into the front seat of his car- "God Speed my dear!" She called back through the opened passenger window, "God Speed! I'll see YOU at 7:30!"

Five blocks of straight lefts and rights, no curves, no lights, just stop signs and one-way streets in perfect grids. She drove past Queen Anne Victorian homes with wide rounded porches, tiny white painted bungalows with brightly colored doors and tall Arts and Crafts homes with stone posts and towering stone chimneys. So many inviting porches, some adorned with fabric bats and melting jack-o-lanterns, others already transitioned to garland and Christmas bows. She checked the address on her sheet affixed to the dash, one more turn, first stop of the day.

They were already waiting outside for her. "Alice and Dave?"

The couple waved and smiled as they walked toward the van. "Get on in! If you don't mind sitting in the back the next person can get in more easily." They didn't mind. They were thrilled to have the ride, explaining Dave's car was in the shop and they couldn't pick it up until Friday when they both got paid.

Carolyn drove the van past the movie theater, past shops and restaurants, the many places that not so long ago, not everyone could go. Past the schools and churches, where not so long ago, not everyone on any given day could enter inside to learn or pray. Past the worn, mowed mound, where hundreds of unnamed souls were buried over a hundred and fifty years ago. Soon the van was full, and she took a direct route to the library so that each of them could do something that not so long ago, was a privilege for some and worth fighting for others. Carolyn patiently waited in the van, flipping through the channels on the old knob dial radio. Country music, rock, Christian rock, rap, country, Christmas music, she laughed as she thought aloud, "As if Americans need early motivation to buy a bunch of crap that nobody wants." Finally, she found her station, *You know, I'm not really sure how I feel about that, I mean come on, I paid good money for my house and I have to think having a prison work crew down the street every day probably wouldn't be the best thing for resale value.* A woman's voice interjected, *they aren't gonna be there*

*forever Joe, you have to look at the facts, these are guys who made mistakes but they aren't violent criminals, they can't be on the crew unless they have an excellent prison record. I'm gonna go against you on this one, everybody makes mistakes, and this is an excellent opportunity for these guys to learn some highly sought after skills.*
Carolyn pulled the ad out of the glove compartment-

Vote Tuesday- Vote Knight for the Right Direction! Gary Knight will bring back the beauty of our town! Knight knows it's Right to keep prisoners in prisons not our neighborhoods. Knight knows it's Right to bring in the businesses you want! Knight knows it's Right to make our parks, streets, and schools safe!

She glared at the old-time picture filled with happy people in her town. Or at least what the town used to look like back when Carolyn was just starting school. Women in fancy dresses holding shopping bags, little boys in little suits and little girls in little fancy dresses, men gathered around cars visiting, everyone wearing a hat. Everyone was white, she scoffed sarcastically, "Bring back the beauty of our town- huf." The woman had finished her rebut, the man announced a caller on the line, *Rob, you're on the air- Hey thanks Joe for taking my call, um, man I'm with Alisia on this one, Knight doesn't give a crap about anyone's house values man. Him and his brother had a contract on that factory with some big hotel developer out east. The artist lady bought the place before they got a closed-door promise on getting the zoning changed. They lost a lot of money to lawyers, man.*

*So, it's a revenge campaign? I mean that's a pretty bad deal, but what about his stance on cleaning up parks and schools, we need that right?*

*God Joe! Do you hear yourself?*

*Yeah Alisia, have you been to the parks? Have you been to Wagon Wheel Park, come on, it's a drug infested hobo tent city.*

*Hey, Joe here again, um, yeah, you watch that park. If Knight wins, I bet there'll be a hotel on it in six months.*

Carolyn quickly pushed the knob turning off the radio. Her guests were on their way back. It wasn't her job to tell them how to vote, it was her job to simply get them there and back home.

They all piled in the same order they originally loaded. Each proudly wearing the bright red, white, and blue I VOTED sticker. Carolyn started up the old van, "Anyone need dropped off somewhere other than home?" Alice responded from the very back, "If you could drop me off at 5ᵗʰ and Oak, I would really appreciate that, my shift starts in twenty minutes." "5ᵗʰ and Oak it is, you know voting day should be a holiday." She would have said more. Had she not signed the *promise not to politicize* volunteer oath that she herself drafted, she would have shared the idea to nix Columbus Day and make it National Voting Day instead. She consoled herself realizing that could wait until 7:30, if anyone hadn't heard her say it already.

Alice stood up and scooted her body sideways past four knees and the middle row of the van, "Thank you so much Carolyn." "No problem and remember to call us again next November if you need a ride." Alice smiled; she knew they might need a ride again. It embarrassed them to have had to call for one in the first place, and yet Carolyn didn't make them feel any different than anyone else. "Hey, wait, how long have you been doing this?" Carolyn gleamed, "Since 1968."

---

The question stuck with her throughout the entire day. Every time she stopped the van and waited, she reflected. She wished Don was with her. She could still see them, fresh out of high school, crammed into the coffee shop, no air conditioning, just fans and opened doors. The kid from her algebra class had just stepped up to the six-inch platform to take a seat in front of the microphone. He picked a few notes and began to sing, *Well it ain't no use to sit an wonder why.....* Carolyn loved Bob Dylan, and the algebra kid did a pretty good rendition. Someone she didn't know jumped up next to him with a harmonica. That was the night she met Don. In a hot coffee shop, drinking hot coffee, singing along to Bob Dylan and Simon and Garfunkel songs. The conversations jaunted back and forth about the war, equal rights, the election. It was Don who said it, that Columbus Day should be nixed for National Voting Day. When the coffee shop closed, they walked and talked until Don suggested he walk her home, somewhere in the range of three in the morning. The chance meeting ended with a plan, a plan to help as many people vote as possible. Don had a car and Carolyn had friends with cars. They never got arrested at a protest like so many of their friends. Never went to Woodstock. Don's hearing caused him to never be drafted. He eventually retired from the Parker Electronics factory. Carolyn worked odd part time jobs and raised their two children. They never did anything anyone considered particularly special, but what they did, they did together and this day, *their* National Voting Day was spent in a car the first Tuesday of November every year since 1968, despite not being old enough to vote. Just once they took a one-hour break, the first Tuesday in November in 1970, to get married, the first year everyone over the age of eighteen could vote. The very first year Don and Carolyn cast their first ballots. At the end of every voting day instead of going to dinner or exchanging expensive presents they gathered back at the coffee shop to watch the election results. They celebrated when their votes resulted in wins and sometimes, they cried when they didn't. Throughout all the decades they saw the pulse of the local elections reach all the way to the White House, an ebb and flow. Fear versus progress, progress redefined.

Carolyn thought about the picture in the ad, how the picture showed such a narrow view of the reality that lay beyond its perfectly cropped borders. The homes that were demolished for parking lots, the people who were intentionally left unrepresented in the photo, the ones who lived in the neighborhoods none of those shoppers would ever go. She thought about the pulse of the day; she could hear the quiet mumblings from the back of the van. Maybe, it was time to retire.

The final polling location stop of the day was always where Carolyn would cast her own vote. Sometimes she would see Don there but only in passing if she did. Just long enough for him to blow her a kiss and mouth the words, "You made it to the moon." The final stop of the day was always the longest.

She parked the van as close to the entrance to the grade school as she could and walked alongside a guest with a broken leg, "I broke it after the absentee deadline." "And that didn't stop you, did it?" He squinted his eyes and smiled, "I would have started walking at noon if you didn't come get me." She understood, she would have done the same.

Once again, the van was packed with people wearing red, white, and blue stickers. Once again, they mumbled and murmured as she drove them each back home through the now darkened streets as a cold north wind poured through the open windows. She was exhausted. 7:27, she was also going to be late.

___

The warm glow of the coffee shop felt as comforting as the warm glow of a fireplace on the coldest winter day. The door made its usual *ding* when she opened it. The shop was packed. Standing room only, except for one chair and a small table covered with a giant anniversary bouquet, directly in front of the six-inch-high stage.

"This way Carolyn! Come on!" The bubbly barista took her hand and led her to the empty chair, sat her down and handed her a cup of coffee. She wanted to ask what was going on, but it was obvious there was no point in asking. The barista started clapping her hands rhythmically, soon the entire room had joined in. Tapping, clapping, absolute silence except for continued tapping and clapping. Don came in through the back door holding his keys in his hands, high into the air. Tapping, clapping. He stepped onto the platform and silence befell the room, "For over fifty years I've spent this day driving a car to make sure as many people can vote as possible. It all started right here in this coffee shop, over fifty years ago when I met this amazing girl. She had short black hair, was wearing a red and tan striped shirt and long tight black slacks- oh how could I forget?" Carolyn blushed as the crowd responded in whoops and hollers. "She lit a fire inside of me to do something that mattered." He choked up a bit, stopping to collect himself. "There were three drivers in 1968 getting citizens to the places they can vote, the places they can participate in the most important privilege we have as citizens, the privilege to participate in DEMOCRACY. Today, we had twenty-two drivers! For over fifty years, I've had a purpose beyond the day-to-day grind of simple existence. For over fifty years, I've had the greatest joy any human being could ask for, and for exactly fifty years that joy has been my inspiration, my wife Carolyn."

Carolyn couldn't speak, but the tears flowing down her cheeks and the smile on her face spoke volumes beyond words. She didn't think, she handed the coffee to the person closest to her and ran to the tiny stage to embrace her beloved partner in their small act of citizenship, her beloved partner in life itself. She could see her two sons, her daughter-in-law, her grandchildren, all of their friends, all of their volunteers. She took a deep breath; they could endure at least one more election.

The barista ceremonially turned on the television, the local news anchor spoke as the election results scrolled along the bottom of the screen. *With only 20% reporting, incumbent Knight is in a dead heat.*

# 12
# December

There was no for-sale sign. Just a small laminated official notice "tax sale." No one ever seems to know how people actually purchase homes this way, but the diligent do. Diligent people like Smith Zimmerman seemed to have a sixth sense in finding penny on the dollar homes before anyone even realized they were technically for sale. Some speculated that he had a full-time staff dedicated to bidding for the best. Some assumed he bought everything he could then sorted it out later. Neither was true. Zimmerman bought at random on nothing more than a gut feeling. In his usual dark blue suit jacket and slick black jeans, he drove through the mid December slush to his final gut-inspired purchase of the year, 1015 Auburn Lane. As with all of Smith's purchases, he never really knew what he was getting into until he broke through the front door. In what time he had to prepare himself before jumping on the purchase he learned as much as anyone could with a computer. Name of most recent owner, virtual map image, liens, anything quick and obvious.

The sun was going down which frustrated him. He had no time to spare, and the crew was on their way to meet him there. No power, no lights. He checked the back seat for flashlights. Three- good but not ideal. Natural light is always best.

The last two turns took his car past a series of small 1940's to 1950's track homes half meticulously kept with Christmas lights draped along porches and holiday yard ornaments in the lawns. The other half were abandoned and boarded with the dead remains of overgrown weeds from at least the previous summer. Some dilapidated with porches filled with roadside couches, bags of trash and windows covered with loosely hung bed sheets. His house, 1015 Auburn Lane was something in between. He never cared to know the story, just the bottom line, how much to make it rentable, how much to make it sellable and which one would bring the most profit.

The *crew* wasn't there. The sun was setting fast. The sad little house began to fade as light slushy snow covered Smith's windshield. He had no time for this, so he reached for his phone.

"Hey man, yeah, we're on our way. Hit a bad wreck on 70. Some jackass decided he could put it in four to beat a tractor trailer. One for the tractor trailer zero for the jackass."

"Crap, okay. I'm not gonna wait for you. I'll be inside."

"You're gonna knock the door down? Have you actually ever done that?"

"Yes, Ron I have." He paused, "Once, but I have and I'm about to do it again."

187

Smith hung up the moment Ron broke out in laughter. Trunk popped, flashlight in hand, he grabbed a crowbar and headed straight for the front door. The hook slipped easily into the door jam, a quick yank...and nothing. The second try created the same result, the third was joined with a swift kick part the way up the door. Smith smiled as the door swung open.

There was just enough daylight left to see his way into the living room and turn on the flashlight. An old harvest green and yellow tweed couch, a coffee table with ends that looked like wagon wheels, a brown faux leather chair, and one laminate end table with a tarnished brass lamp and a yellow faded shade. The entire house was much the same. Simple furnishings, the kind you find at a thrift shop. A hodgepodge of mismatched dishes in the cupboards though nothing out of place. The entire room clean outside of a coffee pot with the remains of two cups of coffee mold in the bottom. The eat-in end of the kitchen revealed three bowls half-filled with cat food and two litter boxes filled with petrified turds.

"Mary loved those cats mister. She really, really did. They were all she had left in the world you know after, well I bet you know already so I won't bore you."

Smith carefully walked back to the living room, "Smith Zimmerman, can I help you?"

A thin older man likely in his 70's stood just inside the doorway. His grey slacks stained and torn, his thick brown bubbly coat half zipped and partly covering a scraggly beard below a baseball cap advertising something Smith had never heard of. "Smith? Zimmerman? Don't know any Zimmerman's. You must be from Mary's mother's side. She said they were mostly in Nebraska. You related to the Dixons? Mary said they were her cousins on that side. I went to school with Lucas Dixon, well he graduated a year ahead of me in 1961, anyway."

"Sir" Smith interrupted, "I have no idea who Mary is, and I am not from here. I'm the new owner of this property, my crew will be here any minute, so I'll have to ask you to leave now. For liability purposes of course."

"Oh, I see. Yes, of course."

Smith opened the door to kindly let the man out, "Oh see, there they are. Thank you for coming by and checking in on the place." The man looked around the house knowing it might be the last time he would see it as it was. You'll put up the decorations, right? She would have wanted that. She loved Christmas as much as she loved those cats."

"We'll see sir. We'll see." The *crew* poured in with Ron at the helm, cigarette dangling from his lips as his eyes squinted, his deeply lined orange face folded from forehead to chin. He made no apology for himself; he was what he was and somehow his rough life worked in tandem with being the leader of the *crew.*

---

Tucked in the center of a row of late 1800's two-story brick Italianates all remaining upright by the existence of each other held the fate of 1015 Auburn Lane. A continuous murmur of conversation, fingers clicking along laptop keys, Indie songs quietly pouring over every inch of the room until someone orders a vanilla latte, and the grinding brings all thought to a short distracting pause. Smith already knew what he would order, a cortado, he already knew where he would sit, the high-top right center, and already had his tablet opened to the spreadsheet filled with addresses. Some sold, some for sale, some rented and only a few vacant. Auburn Lane was unassigned. He passed the window where a woman sat scribbling a black gel pen onto a notebook. He entered as two old friends said good-bye, he got in line as the woman at the counter tried to decide if she wanted to try something new. In the end, she didn't.

"Six grand we get sketchy renters, basically patch the roof, full clean out, fix the garage and the plumbing. Eight grand we get Section Eight, have to add a new stove, a few railings and replace the electric. Kid this one's still running on glass fuses."

"Hey, cut it out with calling me kid, okay?"

"Smith, I'm 50 years old. You're a kid. Just how it is."

"I'll make you a deal, you can call me kid until I'm 35. You have one month, enjoy yourself."

"I'll try to remember that. Anyway, eight grand will get you $900 a month rent, for about fifteen we can sell it for around $120,000. My suggestion is we go with the fifteen, rent it month to month for $950 and put it on the market in April."

"If I agree with you does that validate you calling me kid?"

"Nah, you might be a kid but you're a smart one."

Smith laughed, he liked that. He couldn't help but carry around a bit of pride in being just thirty-four and having purchased forty properties in the previous twelve years. It all began quite accidentally when he bought his first tax sale house when he was just eighteen with the money he got from his high school graduation party. $1,200 for college. He had been accepted to UMKC with the intention of receiving a bachelor's in business but then he met Ron at his part time job at the local hardware store. Ron was in the store almost every day buying paint, nails, grass seed and tools. Smith was Ron's favorite, he seemed to know exactly what Ron was after as if he could read his mind. Ron talked about his investor, what he bought and what he didn't buy. When he told Smith about the tax sale his investor turned down, Smith's gut was born. He faked a family death and sped off to the county courthouse to drop all but $50 of his $1,200 on a 700 square foot bungalow on the west side of Kansas City. He spent three more years working at the hardware store while he fixed the house up himself. In the real estate boom a year later Smith sold the house for $60,000. He personally invited Ron to see it before it closed. From that day on, tax sale investments became an obsession for Smith and a new full-time job for Ron.

"How long?"

"Three, four weeks tops to get it rentable. We'll have to wait until spring to paint the exterior."

"You figure out how to email yet?"

"Look kid," Ron pulled a half-folded stack of notebook paper from his pocket and set it on the table. "It's all itemized here, like it always is. I just can't see the

point in spending a hundred dollars a month on *emailing* you something I can write on two cents worth of paper."

"You got a new key for me?"

Ron reached deeper into his pocket and pulled out a key attached to a rubber held label, 1015 Auburn. "Call me tomorrow and let me know. 35th Street has an inspection tomorrow."

That's how Ron was. Really nothing Smith could do about it. Besides, without Ron the whole thing would fall apart. He hated that. He lived by the ideal that anyone can be replaced. Maybe it was more than the work Ron did, maybe it was a sort of father son kind of deal. Smith never said it. Ron never said it. They both sensed it though and the years they worked together continued to glue the concept into a foundation. He pushed back the thought- he wasn't in business for any sentimental reason, at least he told himself that. No, time was always of the essence, and at this moment time required Smith to once again manually type Ron's chicken scratch into the spreadsheet.

"Mary would appreciate you fixing the house up Mr. Zimmerman. She would have done it herself if she never had, you know."

Smith looked up from the tablet mid type, "No, I'm afraid I don't know. Look mister, I'm afraid you don't understand, I bought the house in the same way I buy any house. It's an investment, I'm fixing it up to rent it or sell it. That's it. I don't know who Mary is and..." He took a breath realizing the man was pained by this Mary he spoke of. He checked his watch, 9:12 am. He didn't have to be anywhere until 10, he had nothing better to do than to listen. At least for a half an hour or so. "I never met Mary, you said something happened to her?" He put the tablet away and waited.

"It was a sad day, my friend. Mary did so well raising those two kids. She worked hard but was always happy. Always so happy. She filled that house with lights and garland and decorations every Christmas. She invited everyone in the neighborhood for Christmas Eve dinner. She had cheese and crackers, cookies, ham, olives, sausage, cakes, fruits, and vegetables...my goodness Smith, people waited all year for it!" He sipped the cup of coffee he had brought with him, "She even had gifts for every child. Every single child. I brought my grandson the year before the accident, for him she gave a puzzle. Just a simple little puzzle but it was of a train. She knew Mr. Zimmerman. She knew he loved trains."

The blender paused the odd conversation. Smith stared at his tablet in anxious anticipation to get back to the work at hand. The noise stopped and he recalled his place in thought, "Tell me about the accident, and please, tell me your name."

"My name?" He laughed, "I didn't realize, yes, I never told you. Benjamin Mercer at your service!" He laughed again. Sipped from the cup and continued, "She worked at the hospital. It was a good job for her. At least she made enough to pay her bills and take care of the kids. Sarah and Alex were in high school when it happened. They were good kids, got good grades and both worked after school. Mary had to stay late because of a bad accident." He stopped and emptied the coffee cup entirely into his mouth. "Maybe she was tired, I don't know, but when she left that night, she ended right back at work as a patient. I heard she was hit by an ambulance. I don't know, all I know is she was never the same after that."

"How long did you know her?"

"Mr. Zimmerman, I can see you are worried about the time. I'll be going now. I would like to come by the house if that's okay."

Smith hadn't expected the abrupt end to Mr. Mercer's story. "Yeah, sure. Anytime Benjamin."

Closings get delayed quite often. Today's closing made Smith anxious; he needed the money to put into Auburn Lane. His one gamble with *sketchy* taught him to never do it again. The three-bedroom two story on 57th street only cost him $3,000 to rent sketchy. Four months later he hadn't seen rent for two months, had $1,200 in fines from the city, almost $500 for the eviction and $7,000 in repairs to make it sellable. The house sat on the market another couple of months and when it finally went under contract it was on an FHA loan, another 30 days to close. The delay came out of final underwriting, which it almost always does. Two deposits in the buyer's bank account that needed verified. Of course, it was a Thursday so of course it would be Monday at the earliest that Smith could close. He picked up his phone to text Ron, silently laughing to himself. *At least Ron texts. Only because I pay for the damn phone, but at least he'll text.*

*Stand down on Auburn, 57th isn't closing today.*

Smith got another cortado, he might as well stay there and finish typing in Ron's estimates. He could go home but there was something pleasant about being surrounded by people. With any amount of focus their words all blended into that soothing background murmur. Even better, none of them wanted to talk to him. He checked his phone, Ron replied. *Take the day off kid. Go get a girlfriend.*

As he typed, his mind wandered. His imagination conjured the image of the Auburn house warm, filled with Christmas decorations and two teenagers waiting for their mom to come home and make sugar cookies. He imagined their devastation when they got the call about the accident. He wondered where they all were now. She had no loan on the house. Surely, she could have kept the taxes up on it, unless of course she died. Even more he wondered why he cared.

Smith looked around the room, the sound began forming into words again. The television silently displayed a news anchor discussing the latest political entertainment as the bottom of the screen scrolled celebrity gossip. An older woman shuffled through the front door, her white hair poking out the edges of an old red and brown stocking cap. A long-oversized winter coat grabbed at every chair she passed until she sat at the table next to Smith. Head down she muddled through a huge cloth bag digging deeper to the bottom to reach a box of random items which soon covered the table. A spoon, a necklace, a child's change purse and a handful of plastic wrapped mints. "Ma'am, would you like a cup of coffee?" Smith always had a soft spot for the lost.

"Yeah. Do you have a cigarette?"

"No."

He brought her the steaming cup and set it next to the necklace. She said nothing, just started drinking. He turned to go back to his table when she called out to him, "Hey. You gonna live in Mary's house? Ben said you got Mary's house."

"No ma'am. I...I'm just fixing it up."

"Oh."

He wanted to leave it at that but the damn image of Mary's house warm and happy wouldn't let him. "Do you know Mary?"

"Of course, I do."

"So, she's alive?"

"Don't know."

"Do you know her children?"

"Don't think so. Mary got sick and the ambulance took her away."

"When did that happen?"

"Umm. It was...it was when she gave me this hat."

The woman took the hat off her head and held it towards Smith.

"I see. That's a very nice hat. You have a good day ma'am."

---

Smith stared at the piece of paper on his square glass coffee table. The giant flat screen television tossed shades of blue across the room as the good guy strapped in arms and ammunition jumped between building tops while the bad guy ran beneath a hovering helicopter. The room shook with the roar of Smith's base-high sound system. He picked the paper up with his left hand and a cold glass bottle of beer with his right.

Grantee: Mary Louise Thomas

Keystone Addition Block 3 Lot 9

May 2$^{nd}$, 1987

He thought about his sister. How much they fought in high school. How much he seemed to always disappoint his father, and how much he took his mother for granted. How much he hated Christmas, all the crap his parents wasted money on just to show off to visitors. How much work went into putting all the lights up outside every November and how much more work it seemed taking them down in January. It was all so formal to him. They bought sugar cookies at the store. They never made them. He wondered if this was the stupid reason he couldn't stop thinking about *Mary's house.* Sugar cookies.

His mind began to fade into sleep, back into the house where Alex and Sarah were helping Mary wrap all the little gifts for the neighborhood kids. He reached for the remote, off and he was out.

---

Fridays are paydays. Smith woke to the sound of Ron beating on his front door. He stumbled off the couch and trod to the door. The sun poured in through every window of the house, "I guess I slept in."

"Guess you did."

Ron walked through the living room straight to the kitchen to start a pot of coffee. "You get a girlfriend yesterday? This place is depressing. You need some art or something. Maybe a vase with fake flowers or animal figurines." He grabbed the sprayer from the sink to fill the back of the coffee maker. "A girlfriend would fix this place up."

"It's called minimalism Ron, and I like it just the way it is."

Smith walked back to his bedroom to get his laptop and checkbook. "Gotta make sure I don't need to make a transfer. I really could have used that closing yesterday."

"You know they'll all be cashed by noon. Dalton's been whining all week about his cable being shut off. And Caleb owes me twenty bucks he borrowed for gas yesterday."

"Let me guess Dalton thinks it's the cable company's fault."

"It always is, isn't it?"

The coffee pot gurgled toward a ten-cup end. Ron already had two of Smiths four coffee cups on the table. "You might want to add some Irish Cream to that. The water line break on 12$^{th}$ Street was a doozy."

Smith never stressed over payday. Was what it was. He would have preferred to pay the crew every other week, but crews live hand to mouth. Things get too tough for them, and they'll quit showing up. Four checks including Ron's, $1,470.

Ron filled both cups, "Tastes weird."

"Highlander Grog, it's my favorite. My sister and her husband got it for me when they went to Scotland last summer."

"Hmm. Anyway, you decided on Auburn?"

"Yeah, yeah we'll go with rentable then sell it."

"Power on?"

"Supposed to be by two today."

"I'll get a roll off over there and we'll start the cleanout this afternoon. Might not finish it."

"That's fine. Can't do much else until I get 57$^{th}$ closed."

Ron grabbed the checks and slammed the rest of the coffee down in his cup, "Tsk, tsk, kid. Get a girlfriend."

---

It was warm. Warm enough to melt all the slush and reveal the salt and mud on Smith's car. The car wash line was twelve cars long. Smith sighed and picked up his phone. "Hey sis."

"Hey big bro. What's up?"

"In line at the car wash"

"So, you only call me when you're bored. I see."

Smith laughed, "Better than never calling at all right?"

"I'll take it. Hey, um I'm just getting ready to walk into a meeting."

"Sure, this won't take long. Do you know how to make sugar cookies?"

"What? Sugar cookies? Okay, yeah you buy them at the store just like good ole' mom."

"I'm serious, I want to make some."

"Like Christmas cookies? You hate Christmas."

"I know. I do. Look it's a long story."

"Google it. I gotta go. Call me later, I wanna hear this story."

"Okay. Talk to you later."


The conversation only got him seventh in line. Normally he would get the inside cleaned but that would take another fifteen minutes. He was anxious to get back to work. Three weeks into the month and he had two tenants still late on rent which warranted a personal visit. He turned onto the highway towards the river, but the turn never happened. Instead, Smith drove himself straight to the hospital.


A kindly old man greeted him in the center of the lobby. "How can I help you today?"

"Where is your records department?"

The old man handed him a map then pulled a sharpie from his red and green holiday vest to circle the destination. "You go straight through this hall then take a left to the elevator. Go to the third floor, first room on the right."

A thick middle-aged woman with dark short curly hair greeted him with much less enthusiasm than the old man. "Can I help you?" She asked as if to say, *please go away.*

"Yeah, um I'm looking for information on a Mary Louise Thomas. She worked here and had an accident at some point. Was hospitalized here."

"Are you family?"

"No."

"Can't help you. That would be a HIPPA violation sir."

Smith walked toward the door. He would have thanked her just like he normally is a great tipper, but she reminded him of the time he left a nickel on the table. An older woman followed him out the door and to the elevator. He could tell she was a cleaning lady by the smock and gloves. When the elevator closed, she tapped his shoulder. "Mary didn't work here. She worked at the old hospital before they tore it down."

"I should have thought of that. Did you work with her in housekeeping?"

"No. Mary was in the cafeteria."

205

Smith felt dizzy. His mind created an impossible thought. "Do you know what happened to her?"

"I better not say. I could get in trouble."

"Do you know if she's alive? Where I could find her?"

"If you go to the soup kitchen on 27th Street, the one by the dog park, you might find her there. I don't know if she's alive. She was last spring. Last I heard."

The elevator opened. "Thank you, ma'am. Thank you so much."

"Good luck and Merry Christmas."

---

It was already 11:30. Smith wound through the old part of town to 27th Street. The soup kitchen entrance had a small awning with the words, *Bowl of Love- Eden House* in the center of a large three-story tan brick building that looked to once be a school. Smith found a parking spot across the street and hurried to the door. He was met with an assumption he had come to volunteer. Carefully hanging his coat and blazer on the hook behind the counter he slipped on the heavy white apron, a pair of clear rubber gloves and stood in front of a massive aluminum pan of mashed potatoes.

The hungry and homeless filed through the line pushing their plastic trays of plate, silverware, and cup along the glass countertop in assembly line fashion. A skinny teenaged boy with half rotten teeth stood to the left of him scooping mixed vegetables onto the plates. To his right a hunched over smiley man with a Veteran's baseball cap ladled light brown gravy to top the potatoes. "DUI?" The skinny boy asked.

"Nope. Just helping out."

"Most people like you had DUI's. I didn't get one. It was something else. Only got twelve more hours left."

"Community Service?"

"That's the deal man."

The veteran intervened, "First time?"

"Yes. Actually, I'm looking for someone. I heard she might be here. Mary Louise Thomas. You know her?"

"I know everyone. I've been volunteering here for twenty years. How do you know Mary?"

"I live in her old neighborhood." It was a real stretch of a white lie, but he went with it.

"She doesn't always make it in. She's real sick you know?"

"I didn't. I heard she wasn't doing well. So, she's alive?"

"Was yesterday. But the day before that someone had a plate made to take to her."

"So, she lives nearby?"

"She lives here. Most of these people do, except of course the homeless."


Two more pans of mashed potatoes and an hour later the kitchen was closed. "Maybe next time kid." Smith didn't even get irritated. He realized he would have called the skinny boy next to him kid. Maybe it was just all relevant to the speaker. Smith reclaimed his blazer and coat. "Come back again" someone called to him as he slowly walked out the door. 1:08 p.m. The crew would be at *Mary's house* in less than an hour. It was only about five blocks away. Rent collection could wait until Monday.


The house still looked sad. Everything looked dirty from the melted snow. Smith fished the key out of the console of the car. The power was on. He sat on the couch and just stared out the window. He pulled his phone from his pocket, he thought *she'll think I'm crazy.* He dialed anyways. "Hey mom. Give me a call when you can. Thanks. Bye."

The screen door creaked as Benjamin walked in. "Mr. Benjamin! I've been waiting for you. Seriously do you watch the house all day?"

"I live across the street. I saw you pull in. Are you going to put up the decorations Mr. Zimmerman?"

"Look Benjamin, I found her. Sort of. At least I know she's alive and where she lives."

"Oh? Well, I coulda told you that but I wasn't sure if I outa. I go see her every Sunday afternoon. Me and the Misses that is."

"Please tell me, where are her children?"

"They're around. Mr. Zimmerman, I told you it all went bad after the accident. The doctors gave her the pills and when they took them away from her... Well, it destroyed Alex and Sarah. She wrote bad checks, she lost her power, she used up her savings. The kids tried to help but they couldn't. They walked away, it made it easier that way. Just pretended like she was dead."

"But she's sick. Do they know she's sick?"

"No. I doubt it. She ended up in a halfway house last spring. She got better, well you know, got off the junk. She said the kids changed their phone numbers. Her son lives not too far from here still, but he refuses to talk to anyone about her. I went to his work to tell him she was sick and when he found out I was there he left. That's how it is."

"How sick is she?"

"Cancer Mr. Zimmerman. Nothing they can do. That's why we go every Sunday now. It won't be long."

Smith's phone rang. "Excuse me." He walked into the kitchen. "Hi mom."

"Smith, are you okay?"

"I think so. Yeah, I just, I had a weird question. When dad was in the hospital, I think I was six right?"

"Yeah, it was Christmas time, so you were almost seven. What about it?"

"Do you remember sending me to the cafeteria to get you a cup of coffee?"

"Not really but I'm sure I did. You were probably keeping your dad from sleeping. No, I do remember. I sent you to the cafeteria several times. You were a chatter box!"

"I thought I remembered that."

"In fact, I do remember now. Every time you came back with whatever I sent you for you had a sugar cookie."

"She said her little boy was about my age."

"Who said that? Smith, are you okay?"

"I gotta go mom. I'll call you later."


He put the phone back in his pocket and opened the door off the kitchen to the garage, "Benjamin, you coming? Let's find those decorations."


Benjamin met him in the basement. "Sure enough, it's all right here."

"So, you will put them up?"

"Can you bring her here? Can you bring Mary here on Christmas Eve?"

"Sure, the wife and I take her places all the time."

"If she had a nurse, a helper, could she live on her own?"

"Well, yeah. She already has one Mr. Zimmerman."

"Can she walk okay?"

"Not anymore. They got her a nice wheelchair though. And on her good days she uses a walker."

Smith could hear the crew bumbling around upstairs. He quickly grabbed a handful of decorations and ran back up the stairs, through the garage and into the kitchen. "Where you want us to start boss?" Dalton stood lumbering in the middle of the living room staring around the place trying to decide what he would be taking home with him.

Smith handed him the decorations. "Get these up. There's more in the basement. Caleb clean the place up, vacuum, dust, regular cleaning. The rest of you go get some plywood and make a ramp on one end of the porch.

"Kid, have you lost your ever-loving mind?"

"No Ron. I'll explain it later."

"So, we're not renting it?"

"Not right now."

Benjamin made it up the stairs and back into the kitchen. Smith pulled a hundred-dollar bill out of his pocket. "Can you invite the neighbors? Monday night five p.m. Get the kids presents; the same kind of little stuff Mary would get. Can you do that for me?"

Benjamin stood up as straight as his body would allow and gave a salute, "Yes sir!"

"I gotta go guys. We have until Monday night to get this all done. So, no messing around."

"Whatever you say boss."

"He's gone nuts."

"My wife's gonna love this one."

Smith walked through the grocery store with his phone propped up in the baby seat of the shopping cart. *Flour, sugar, butter, eggs, vanilla, baking powder and baking soda.* He stopped at the deli counter, "What can I get you today?" a small petite high school aged girl from behind the counter asked him. "Yes, I need to make a delivery order for Monday." She grabbed a pen and notepad on a shelf behind her, "Ready!"

"Um, let's do two veggie trays, two fruit trays, a dessert tray, sliced ham, oh a relish tray."

"How much ham?"

"A big one".

"Oh. Okay. Anything else?"

"Yeah, can you make a cake and deliver it also?"

The girl looked confused. "A cake? I'm sorry, no one ever asked that. Hold on, I'll get my manager. It'll just take a second."

She returned less than a minute later with her manager, who kindly took over the order sheet, "I think we can make you a cake sir. What size?"

"Round? Big, make it a big round one with two layers."

The manager scribbled on the pad, "And what flavor?"

"Gosh, I don't know. Let's make it simple, vanilla. All vanilla, frosting too."

"And do you want any words on it?"

"Yeah, have it say, *Welcome home Mary.*"

"All-righty, got it. What's the address?"

"1015 Auburn Lane."

The man tore the paper off the pad. "What time?"

"Five p.m. Monday." The girl grabbed the paper, "I work Monday, I can deliver it."

"You know, this is actually on my way home. I got this one, Kayla. Anything else?"

"Just one thing, do you guys sell cookie sheets?"

---

Smith had the stereo on full blast. This time his phone was propped up on the edge of a book on the kitchen counter. He didn't think about needing a bowl or a wooden spoon. Instead, he mixed the ingredients in his largest pot, stirring them with a bread knife. "One egg." He cracked the egg into a bowl realizing there were eleven left. He'd have to eat eleven eggs at some point. Smith almost never cooked. Reaching for a fork to whip the egg his phone rang. "Sis! Hey!"

"Open the door. I'm at your front door. I've been knocking for five minutes."

Julia walked in on a mission starting with turning the music down. "Mom called me, she's worried about you."

"I'm fine sis. Sit down. You can watch me make sugar cookies."

Julia nabbed a beer from the refrigerator and took a seat at the kitchen table. "Sugar cookies. Seriously Smith, what is going..." Suddenly she snapped back from the table. "Smith!! Okay, what's her name? Tell me right now, what's her name?"

"It's a he, Julia. That's a boy cat, his name is Smokey. That's what the shelter said anyways."

"No, what's *her* name. Come on, you obviously have a girlfriend. You have a cat and you're making sugar cookies. So just tell me, what's her name?! Besides, I thought you hated Christmas, and thought cats were stupid."

"None of this is actually about Christmas, I'm still not a fan. As for the cat, I kind of like him. Look, I wish I had that easy of an out on this. No girlfriend. Hey, look at my phone please, what comes after the egg?"

Julia had stopped petting the happy purring cat on her lap and grabbed the phone, "Vanilla. One teaspoon. Do you actually own measuring spoons?"

Smith laughed, "Yeah, I actually do! Mom got them for me when I moved in. Spoons and cups. No mixing bowls or wooden spoons though. I improvised."

"I see that. So fine, no girlfriend. What's the deal?"

"Remember when dad was in the hospital. When he had the heart attack?"

"No. I was like four. I remember the story though, so what about it?"

"Mom took me with her every day to visit him. We stayed most of the day. You were there too, but you were good and quiet, and I wasn't so mom kept sending me to the cafeteria to get her stuff. A cup of coffee, a glass of juice, a sandwich, stuff like that. Anyway, every time I got her something the lady at the cafeteria gave me a sugar cookie. I remember she told me that *her own little boy was about my age.* Julia, I bought her house and she's dying."

"I'm gonna need another beer for this."

---

Monday morning started with a call from Smith's closer. "Good news, we're clear to close. Docs are on their way. Can you meet me at Homeland Title at four?"

217

"I can close before they do, can we get this done before noon?"

"Yeah, we might have to do it off location. I can do it though. I'll call you when I know what time."

"Great. Thank you."

Smith was at the house by nine. The crew was there working on the ramp and putting up the decorations. Benjamin and his wife came over with the wrapped gifts as soon as they saw Smith pull into the drive.

"We have ten children coming Mr. Zimmerman! Betty, you put 'em all under the tree okay?" Betty nodded and began carefully stacking the gifts below the old fake tree that probably hadn't left the basement in at least ten years.

Smith looked around the house, it looked perfect. "Benjamin, this what it looked like when Mary did it?"

"Pretty much, I think. I don't remember exactly where everything was but I'm sure she'll love it."

Smith's phone beeped a reminder, *ten-thirty, coffee shop.*

"Ron!"

"I'm right here kid." Ron popped out of the bathroom into the hallway. "I don't know what the hell you're doing or why the hell your doin' it, but I figured if you wanted a ramp, I should make the bathroom handicapped too."

"Dude! Yes! I didn't even think of that. Hey, we're closing on 57ᵗʰ in half an hour. I have to grab something from my car really quick, make sure the boys keep the front door shut."

Smith came back in with a bag of cat food, a bowl, a litter box, and Smokey.

---

He was early. He got his usual and even was able to get the center high top. "We close at two, you know for Christmas Eve." The barista almost seemed sad to go home early.

Isabell came in with a manila envelope tucked under her arm. Her dishwater blonde hair pulled into a ponytail wrapped bun. Her long black trench coat dripping from cold winter rain. "Would you rather it was snow?"

"Geeze, I don't know. It is Christmas Eve so it would be movie perfect."

"Liz, thank you for taking this one. I don't know what I'm gonna do without you."

"You'll be just fine. I'm leaving you in good hands." She pulled a pen from her purse and dumped the contents of the envelope on the table.

"So, it's really going that well? It really worked?"

"It really is, Smith! I've never been happier in my life. Mira and I are adding organic micro-greens and sweet potatoes next spring. All together we already have almost two dozen restaurant contracts!"

"I'm really happy for you. Seriously, I want to visit the farm next year. Maybe you can teach me something. I even tried my hand at baking the other night."

"We'd love to have you visit the farm. Baking huh? What did you bake Mr. Zimmerman?"

"Sugar cookies. They aren't good but they aren't terrible."

Smith signed the papers. He was finally done with 57ᵗʰ St.

"I'm going to run these back to the office, I'll text you after they close but the wire probably won't hit until Wednesday."

"That's fine. Seriously. Hey if you and Tom can, I'm hosting a Christmas party at 1015 Auburn Lane tonight. You guys should come by."

"You're hosting a Christmas party?"

"Long story."

"I'll try. Merry Christmas, Smith."

---

The house was spotless. It was warm and filled with decorations. Benjamin found a radio in the garage and had it playing a local Christmas station. Doyle even went to the store and bought coffee grounds. Cheap coffee grounds, but there was coffee, nonetheless. By 4:30 everything was ready. Julia arrived at 4:45 with a box of sugar cookies. "Bro, they weren't terrible but..."

4:50 sharp Benjamin and Betty arrived. He carefully pulled the wheelchair from the trunk, set it on the sidewalk and pulled it apart. Locked the brakes and opened the back-seat door. Betty helped the frail woman into the chair. Smith wanted to run out to greet her, but he reminded himself, this was about her, not him. Instead, he waited at the door for them to arrive.

"Welcome home Miss Mary."

The woman in the chair hardly resembled the one who had given him the cookies so many years before, hardly but enough so that her warm smile brought a flashback that confirmed it was definitely her. She was weak, and it was obvious the *junk* had almost got her. But she was clean. Dying but clean. "Smith, I don't know how a few cookies got me back in my home but I....," She wiped away the tears, "This is an answer to prayers."

Smith ran to the kitchen and grabbed Smokey from his food dish, "Here Mary, this is Smokey. He's yours."

She pulled the cat onto her lap, petting him and telling him what a pretty boy he was. She didn't have long to visit with him before the neighbors began pouring in.

They brought gifts and pictures. Twenty years' worth of pictures of Christmas Eve at Miss Mary's. Then the doorbell rang.

When Smith opened the door, the deli manager stood before him with a giant two-layer vanilla cake which read *Welcome Home Mary* in red and green frosting just like he asked for. He walked inside and set the cake down on the coffee table directly in front of Mary herself. Instead of standing up and returning to bring in the rest of the

food, he knelt down on the living room floor. He stared into Mary's eyes. As a single tear slipped from his own, his crackled voice uttered one little word, "Mom."

# Epilogue

Each tale came from a question, a concern, an angst, a joy, or an inspiration that quickly invited characters to play out their own stories.

January-

It seems that every generation complains about the generations that follow. Then again, we have a culture of complaining in general. The idea that any generation would question the decades old adherence to *the order of things* seems to be at the heart of hostility towards so many Millennials. As a mother of Millennials, I celebrate the challenge this generation has presented. Having even a portion of our society less obsessed with consumerism meant to impress everyone around them at the expense of living meaningful lives could be the best thing that ever happened to us.

February-

I read *The Catcher in the Rye* by J.D. Salinger from a large boulder on the Colorado River somewhere between Meeker and Rifle when I was sixteen years old. It was an AP English requirement to read it and *The Bell Jar* by Sylvia Plath before school started in the fall. I didn't love the book (although I didn't feel like I needed emergency therapy unlike my mental response to *The Bell Jar*). I was however intrigued that Salinger wrote something so timeless, popular, and controversial. A few years ago, I watched a documentary on Salinger, and although I have no idea how accurately it portrayed his life and personality, I had to wonder what a female author of a *one-hit-wonder* might behave like. Soon, a Miss Eliza Manning, awkward and nearly agoraphobic entered the stage.

March-

A very real and very lonely-looking dog on his way to nowhere stole my heart one day. He refused to leave my mind in a sort of parental way. As a proud shelter-dog mom (and a few grand-dogs) I had to create a scenario where someone found him, took him home and loved him. This story is for my brother Patrick Gene Emrick who spent his short thirteen years trying to save every animal he ever came across. Please support your local shelter and if you decide it's time to bring a fur baby home, there is nothing more rewarding than adding a new family member that without you may have never had a home, or your love.

April-

While attending a presentation at the 2018 Missouri Main Street Conference in St. Louis, I heard a poignant statement that I knew to be true although not often enough talked about. So often, when we see a locally owned business shutter in less than a few years of opening we place blame on everything except reality. We cling to our chain stores and big box conglomerates while insisting that locally owned downtown businesses are *doomed* to failure. Spending time AND money at locally owned businesses in historic downtowns is an experience that has become nostalgic, fun, and desired in a world filled with brown and tan boxes. Finding capital, dealing with zoning (which has been in favor of chain stores for decades) and paying high taxes make it tough to make this American Dream a successful endeavor. The facts, however, prove that locally owned businesses and historic preservation have a massive economic benefit to your community. To learn more, check out these fantastic resources:

MainStreet.org

PlaceEconomics.com

MichaelhShuman.com

May-

The year 2020 proved how fragile the world's supply chain is, and most importantly how unsustainably we source our food. In the same way the oil embargo of the early 1970's spurred a short-term movement of growing our own food, the COVID pandemic has spurred on a similar response. I encourage people to grow their own food, it is a rewarding and tasty activity. Unfortunately, it will only make a tiny dent in solving the bigger problem and most of us can't grow all of the food we eat. Support local restaurants that source locally grown food. If you have a farmers' market, go there, and go there often!

June-

Homelessness is on the rise, and it is everywhere. According to the United States Department of Housing and Urban Development, over 580,000 people in our country were homeless in 2020. That is an increase of nearly 13,000 people from 2019. The same policies and procedures being enacted over and over are obviously still not working. Opal's ideas may not be the answer, but they are outside of the box, and in that space, we are more likely to find real solutions. Sometimes, it is difficult to consider solutions that look very differently than the one's we've been hoping for.

July-

We all must cross that point where it feels like we're making a commitment to a lifelong occupation. Being exceptionally good at something doesn't always equate to actually enjoying it.

Deciding what you want to do for the rest of your life at seventeen or eighteen years old is a tremendous challenge, especially when there is pressure to go one specific direction. As parents, we *want* what is best for our children, although we *don't* always know what that is.

Also, July is not the best month to plant a garden in Missouri although it can be done with a little extra care and quite a bit extra watering. It just so happened that July was the only month that would work for Gretel to fulfil Anabelle's sacrificed dream of a little garden park.

August-

There are public servants that devote their lives to what is in their hearts, even if you don't agree with them. And then... there are politicians. Both can have the same titles.

September-

After one of dozens of trips to Kirksville, MO, I came home filled with absolute awe of the natural landscape of Missouri in September. I wrote a poem, and ode if you will, of gratitude to live in such a beautiful place. September often brings the first respite from long hot and humid summers. Those 70-something degree days are the beginning of my favorite season of the year. In an almost transcendental way, there is a sense of peacefulness that overcomes you.

October-

The Mountain Lion or North American Cougar is officially a non-Missouri resident despite everyone knowing someone who claims to have seen one. According to the Missouri Department of Conservation, most sightings are actually large house cats or bob cats seen from a distance. Some cougar sightings have been confirmed as either escaped cats from private ownership or cats moving through in migration. Either way, if you've ever heard one *scream*, you'll never forget it. To learn more, go to mdc.mo.gov

November-

American women received the right to vote in 1920, Native Americans in 1924 and Black Americans in 1965. There will always be challenges to democracy and there will always be those who play their part to meet those challenges.

"Never doubt that a small group of thoughtful, committed citizens can change the world. Indeed, it's the only thing that ever has."[1] Margaret Mead

---

[1] Nancy C. Lutkehaus, *Margaret Mead: The Making of an American Icon* (Princeton, NJ: Princeton University Press, 2008), p. 261

December-

I love the timeless classic *A Christmas Carol,* by Charles Dickens and although quite by accident, this story is in some ways a modern, more realistic version. In my mind, Smith Zimmerman became the character meant to meet Mary. He was no Scrooge, as I don't believe there are very many humans that misanthropic. He also doesn't experience an overnight transition becoming an entirely different person. He does, however, create a solid way to introduce a story that is all too common in the era of opioid addiction. According to the United States Health and Human Services, $2/3^{rd}$ of 760,000 drug overdoses since 1999 were from opioids[2]. Many of these were addictions formed from doctor prescribed opioids. Most of us have seen a "Mary," but most of us have no idea what got that person to where they are. A little love and compassion can go a long, long way.

---

[2] "Opioid Crisis Statistics," U.S. Department of Health and Human Services, last modified February 12, 2021

# About the Author

Audrey Elder is a historic researcher and amateur homesteader. She is author of *Guide to Selling Historic Properties*, and teaches continued education for Missouri and Kansas real estate agents.

Audrey writes and provides educational presentations about environmental sustainability, historic preservation, and conscious living. Elder lives on 14 acres in northwest Missouri with her husband Dan and several million honeybees.

Her blogs can be found at Meaningful-Living.org, FourteenAcreWood.com and AudreyLElder.com

# Publications by HearthMasters Publishing

January Through December: Twelve Short Stories – One
Coffee Shop by Audrey L. Elder 2021

The Chimney and Hearth Pro's Resource Book
By Marge Padgitt 2010-2021

Wood-Fired Heating and Cooking by Marge and Gene
Padgitt 2021

The Fireplace Manual by Marge Padgitt (coming soon)

The Lombardo Family History and Cookbook
By Marge Padgitt and Family 2021

Historic Chimney Restoration by Marge and Gene
Padgitt 2022

The publisher is seeking submissions by authors

HearthMasters Publishing
A division of HearthMasters, Inc.
PO Box 1166
Independence, MO 64051
www.hearthmasters.net
816-461-3665